Trail of Secrets

Laura Wolfe

F&I
by Melange Books

Published by
Fire and Ice
A Young Adult Imprint of Melange Books, LLC
White Bear Lake, MN 55110
www.fireandiceya.com

Trail of Secrets ~ Copyright © 2015 by Laura Wolfe

ISBN: 978-1-68046-155-8

Published in the United States of America.

Cover Art by Caroline Andrus

For Chewy
2005-2015

Chapter One

Footsteps pounded faster, closing in on her. Brynlei darted off the rocky path and squeezed between the trees, her arms outstretched to feel through the darkness. A stray branch sliced into the side of her face, but she forced her way through the brush, no longer certain what direction she was heading. She clamored down a steep embankment, her knees buckling and hands pushing away the wet earth, willing herself to get back up. The truth dangled in front of her like a low-hanging star, but the odds of her living to tell anyone about her discovery were shrinking with every footstep crashing behind her.

Just before the hands grabbed her in the dark and wrestled her to the ground, a cyclone of thoughts reeled through Brynlei's mind. Her cabin mates sleeping comfortably in their bunks. The void of Anna's absence beside her. The golden notes of music floating from Rebecca's violin. The buttery-sweet scent of her mom's oatmeal cookies baking in the oven. Her wonderfully boring life back in Franklin Corners. Lastly, she pictured each word printed in the glossy pages of the Foxwoode Riding Academy brochure and almost laughed at its false advertising, its glaring omissions. Nowhere in the crisp twenty-page packet was there any mention of Caroline Watson, the fifteen-year-old girl who went out on a trail ride four years earlier. And never returned.

* * * *

Three Weeks Earlier

Brynlei placed her muddy paddock boots on the mat in the garage before stepping onto the laundry room floor. The glistening white tiles

1

appeared freshly mopped, as usual, and Brynlei knew better than to be the one to mess it up. The family's golden retriever, Maverick, bounded toward her, wagging his long, shaggy tail and sniffing her pant legs. She scratched the soft spot behind his ears, as Maverick leaned into her and closed his eyes. Her mom was baking scones in the oven, and the ingredients hit Brynlei's nose in layers. First the lemon, eggs, sugar, and lavender, and then a hint of something else. Maybe coriander? She wondered if Maverick smelled the coriander too. She'd read that dogs smelled things in much the same way.

"Did you add coriander this time?" Brynlei said.

Her mom held the broomstick away from her body, as she halted mid-sweep and stared at Brynlei. "Just a tablespoon. Thought I'd add another twist to the recipe."

Her mom's hair was pulled smoothly back into a low ponytail and she wore her black and white checked apron over her button-down shirt and khaki pants. The apron, which read *Jackie's Bakery* in cursive letters across the chest, had been a gift from Brynlei and her older brother, Derek, last Christmas.

The granite counters in the kitchen gleamed in spite of the baking that had recently taken place. Brynlei would have been sure her mom was Martha Stewart in a past life, except that Martha Stewart was still alive.

"How was your ride?"

"Good." Brynlei could have told her about Rosie taking longer than normal to warm up, her trot unusually stiff as they tracked left. Or about Teri setting the jumps higher than last week, at 3'3". Or about the nearly flawless course she'd ridden, but she was too nervous about tomorrow to engage in unnecessary talking. Her mom didn't understand much about the nuances of riding anyway.

Brynlei sat down at the kitchen table and picked up the Foxwoode Riding Academy brochure. She flipped through its pages for the thousandth time. The brochure felt fancy and important, with its spiral binding and heavy-duty cardstock. Not like the flimsy catalogs that arrived daily in the mail. She had memorized every page, as if she'd taken a picture of each bit of information and filed it away in her brain. Each photograph, paragraph, sentence, and word was ingrained in her mind's eye. Brynlei could also remember courses she'd jumped three years ago in riding lessons and pages of books she'd read, word for word. She'd heard people refer to her memory as "photographic", but she wasn't sure she had that ability. She could only keep mental pictures of things that were important to her. Although she could view the catalog in her mind, she couldn't stop herself from looking at the real thing again. "Students ride up to four hours a day with instruction from expert riders at the top level of the sport," boasted page two. Vibrant photos pictured professional-looking horses and riders jumping over a variety of colorful obstacles. Page three highlighted amenities, including "access to the crystal blue waters and sandy beaches of Lake Foxwoode, a dining hall with gluten-free and vegan meal options, a tennis court, and hundreds of acres of riding trails."

Brynlei had read the brochure so many times in the last few months that the edges of the pages were ripped and worn, despite the high quality paper. Page nineteen of the brochure stated that each year Foxwoode awarded "a fully-paid scholarship to one deserving equestrian who was in need of financial assistance." Finally, page twenty outlined Foxwoode's strict code of conduct, assuring parents that their daughters would be safely returned "with new friends, improved riding and horsemanship skills, and summer memories from northern Michigan that will last a lifetime."

"Are you finished packing?" her mom asked.

"Almost," Brynlei said. "I need to clean my boots, and I'm going to call Rebecca to say goodbye." Brynlei's three-week session at Foxwoode Riding Academy started tomorrow.

She pressed Rebecca's name on her phone and waited for the familiar voice to answer.

"Hey. What's up?"

"Just wanted to say bye. You'll probably miss me."

"Um, yeah. I'll miss your face. That's for sure. Have fun at your fancy hunt club." Rebecca spoke with her best British accent.

"Have fun at your fancy violin club," Brynlei replied.

Rebecca was leaving for music camp at Interlochen in a few days.

"Text me as soon as you get back."

"I will. Unless I get discovered and run off to Europe. Then you'll never hear from me again."

"Sounds good."

"Bye."

Brynlei and Rebecca Adler had been best friends since the first day of second grade at Birchwood Elementary. She had often wondered if their teacher, Mrs. Miller, was aware that her seemingly random assignment of seats would result in a lifelong friendship. Sitting at her assigned table, Brynlei's freshly-trimmed bangs and crisp blue jeans had suddenly felt plain next to Rebecca, with her cascading auburn hair, violet dress, and sparkling silver shoes that matched the glistening buttons on her sleeves. Rebecca lunged for some scissors and paper and began to cut shapes out of construction paper, per Mrs. Miller's instructions, but Rebecca's scissors would not cut the paper. She gripped, maneuvered, tugged and turned, but the scissors wouldn't cut. Brynlei stared at her orange piece of paper, pretending not to notice, until Rebecca turned to her.

"My scissors aren't working."

She lent Rebecca her scissors, but those didn't work for Rebecca either. Then Brynlei noticed the scissors in Rebecca's left hand.

"You need lefties," Brynlei had said to her.

"Oh, yeah," Rebecca responded, as if she had completely forgotten that she was left-handed. They had both unleashed an outburst of laughter that nearly caused Brynlei to fall out of her chair. It was only when Mrs. Miller threatened to move their seats that they'd managed to regain their composure.

She and Rebecca had been inseparable ever since. Things were easy with Rebecca. Rebecca could glide through any social situation like a butterfly flittering from flower to flower. When Brynlei froze up in front of people, cotton balls filling her mouth, Rebecca stepped up and shot out one-liners that invariably made people laugh or, at least, back off. Most importantly, Rebecca knew everything about Brynlei.

Brynlei always looked forward to eating Chinese carryout with Rebecca and her parents on Friday nights. Spending time at the Adler's house was like being on vacation. Their house had a different texture than hers. The colors were more vibrant, the noises sharper, the food spicier. It was like her own private carnival—colorful, fun, and unexpected. She never had to guess what Rebecca or her parents were thinking. Brynlei could sit in the Adler's living room for hours listening to Rebecca play her violin, each luscious note dripping off the next and melding like liquid gold.

When she was with Rebecca, things were never boring. That said a lot coming from the sleepy Detroit suburb of Franklin Corners. Every Christmas, Rebecca presented Brynlei with an outrageous present, like the Mexican horse Chia Pet she'd received last year. In exchange, Brynlei always chose eight small Hanukkah gifts to give to Rebecca, a different theme each year. Eight bottles of nail polish, each a different color. Eight exotic fruits that they'd never eaten before. Rebecca relished the guessing game.

"Is it eight brands of ibuprofen? Eight varieties of light bulbs? Oh, I know, eight meatless toppings for my chilidog."

There was no question that Rebecca had been a comedian in a past life.

Although it seemed childish now, Brynlei remembered the summer after fourth grade when she'd convinced Rebecca to join her Horse Lover's Club It was not lost on Brynlei that Rebecca had not actually "loved" horses or even particularly liked them. She had always been terrified of horses, but she played along.

They set up Brynlei's room to look like a giant horse stall, spreading yellow clothes and towels all over the floor. When Brynlei's mom walked in with a horrified look on her face, they had yelled, "That's the hay!" and laughed until Brynlei couldn't breathe.

Leaving for Foxwoode without Rebecca felt like someone had chopped off her right arm just before hurling her through Foxwoode's front gate. She wanted to focus on riding and not waste all of her energy trying to make friends. Rebecca knew about Brynlei's diagnosis from the psychologist. Brynlei didn't feel like explaining to people she didn't know why she wore synthetic riding boots instead of leather ones, or why loud noises sent her running for cover. It was all so exhausting. It would be so much easier to let Rebecca do the dirty work, as she'd always done. Rebecca would make the introductions, crack a joke, and forge new friendships while Brynlei coasted in her wake. Rebecca didn't ride and Brynlei did. She would have to quiet the voices in her head and try to fit in with the girls at Foxwoode on her own.

Chapter Two

After five hours in the car with her parents, Brynlei almost jumped through the window of their Ford Explorer when she finally spotted the entrance to Foxwoode. They nearly sped past the crooked plywood sign that hung from a tree on the side of the road. Brynlei would have missed the sign altogether, except for the word "Foxwoode" scrawled across it in bright white paint. The sign appeared to have been assembled by a Kindergartner.

"There it is! Don't miss the turn!"

Brynlei's dad slammed on the brakes when Brynlei yelled.

In truth, Brynlei had expected a more stately entrance to the fancy riding academy. Yet, sure enough, the sign said *Foxwoode*.

"Is this right?" her mom asked. "It's not very well marked."

"I'll just turn and see where it takes us," Brynlei's dad said. He steered off the two-lane country road past the homemade sign and onto a narrow dirt road enveloped by towering pine trees. Clouds of dust surrounded the windows as the SUV ambled over rocks and potholes.

"This can't be right." Brynlei's mom clutched the armrest while she bounced in her seat.

Brynlei searched through the murky dust for any sign of horses or cabins or girls, but only saw trees. Then she spotted another lopsided wooden sign with the same white lettering that read *Service Road – Employees Only*.

"Looks like we turned a little early," her dad said. Sweat glistened on his scalp through his dark, thinning hair.

"I knew this couldn't be right," Brynlei's mom said. "Find a place to turn around, Dan."

Brynlei held onto the door handle and tensed her muscles every time the SUV hit another pothole and knocked her off-balance. They ambled along the one-lane path, searching for a place to turn.

"It's too narrow for a U-turn," her dad said. "I have to keep going until the road widens."

Her mom let out a deep, disapproving sigh.

"Someone needs to pave this sucker," her dad said, trying to lighten the mood.

Sometimes Brynlei felt sorry for her dad, always having to balance out her mom's expectations of perfection. Brynlei had been shocked by photos she'd seen of her parents in their younger days, before Derek was born. They appeared carefree and happy, like they were on a never-ending quest for fun. In one photo in particular, her dad was almost unrecognizable. She could only describe him as shockingly handsome, with thick dark hair and tanned skin. Her mom posed next to him showing off her perfectly trim body in a mini-skirt and high-heels. They smiled at each other in the photo in a way that Brynlei didn't see much anymore, as if they shared the punch-line to an inside joke that no one else could possibly understand. Did her parents remember how they'd felt at that moment? Brynlei wouldn't be surprised if they had forgotten.

With no other option, Brynlei's dad continued driving down the narrow dirt road. Brynlei hoped a wide-open area would appear as they rounded each bend, but each time she was disappointed.

"This is ridiculous," her mom said. "How do they expect people to turn around?"

Through the mesh of trees, Brynlei made out a small cabin in the distance. No, it wasn't a cabin; it was more like an open-air shed that was being used to store tools and equipment. The dark figure of a person appeared next to the shed. A wave of static electricity jolted through Brynlei, making it impossible for her to breathe. She wasn't sure why she was picking up on this sudden surge of energy. She tried to get a better look to see if the person was an employee or a maybe another riding student, but the dense trees passing outside the car window obstructed her view.

"There's someone over there, by that shed." Brynlei finally coughed up the words. "We can ask them how to get out of here."

"I don't see anyone," Brynlei's mom said.

Brynlei looked again. The person she'd seen just moments ago was gone. She lowered her window and craned her neck outside to get a better view, but still could not see anyone. She scanned the trees, dumbfounded. Maybe the person was behind the shed? Or inside it?

"Here we go," Brynlei's dad exclaimed. A grassy meadow crisscrossed with tire tracks appeared on the side of the road. Obviously, they weren't the first ones to turn around here. As they headed back down the narrow dirt road in the other direction, Brynlei peered through her window hoping to catch a glimpse of whomever she had seen. However, the only activity in the woods came from a couple robins flitting about and a chipmunk scurrying up the massive trunk of an oak tree.

Ten minutes later and two miles down the country highway, they arrived at Foxwoode's proper entrance. Brynlei recognized the impressive gated entrance flanked by limestone pillars from page two of the brochure. A wave of competing emotions rushed through her— excitement, nervousness, fear of the unknown. Brynlei squeezed her hands into fists and drew in her breath while her stomach flopped around like a fish caught in a net.

"This looks more like it," her dad said.

"We'll never make that mistake again." Brynlei's mom pulled a compact from her purse and patted the shine off her nose.

* * * *

They checked in at the office where an overly-friendly woman directed them to Cabin 5. The sun reflected off the silver Explorer, as Brynlei's parents unloaded the last of her bags. The cabin appeared exactly as the cabins pictured in the brochure, with its rustic log walls, high ceilings, and a narrow hallway leading to a communal bathroom. The smell of cedar, granola bars, and lemon-scented cleaning product clung to Brynlei's nose. Four of the six bunks had already been made up and a few suitcases lined the walls, their owners nowhere to be found. Brynlei eyed the one remaining bunk and tossed her stack of sheets on the lower bed.

"This place isn't too shabby," her dad said. He carried a large pink suitcase through the cabin door. "It smells kind of funny, though."

"You mean like horses?" Brynlei said.

She'd thought her dad's jokes were funny when she was younger, but they didn't have the same effect anymore. That didn't stop him from trying, though. His searching eyes revealed his disappointment at the cabin devoid of girls and their parents. Dan Leighton was most comfortable chatting up total strangers about the Tigers or the weather before leading into his usual talk of office buildings for sale and lease. He was the head of his own commercial real estate company and was rarely able to turn off his quest to find new clients. Apparently, he'd arrived on this earth innately wired to network with people. Brynlei guessed her dad had been the head of a commercial real estate company in his past life, too. She couldn't think of anything she'd want to do less.

Her mom smoothed out the sheets and blankets and tucked them under the foot of the bunk bed. In one swift motion, she sealed up everything tight with crisp hospital corners. Then she fluffed the pillow and centered it on the bed.

"There. Just like at home." Brynlei's mom pressed her lips into a thin smile. "Remember to wash your sheets at least once."

"I know, Mom," Brynlei replied.

She caught a glimpse of herself in the full-length mirror that hung on the cabin wall. In contrast to her mom's polished exterior, Brynlei sometimes startled herself with her plainness. Not that she was unattractive. Her shoulder-length hair was somewhere between light brown and dirty blond, but it was smooth and shiny. Her dark eyes were large and round. Girls at school often hinted at her redeeming features, but they usually said it in a way to suggest she could do more. "Your hair is so pretty. You should try wearing it in a braid sometime." Or "You have beautiful eyes. A little bit of eyeliner would really make them pop." They didn't understand that she'd rather blend in, and blending in came effortlessly to her. Besides, the horses didn't care what she looked like.

"Let's go find some of your cabin mates so you can introduce yourself," her mom said.

"Great idea," her dad chimed in. "I'll try not to embarrass you." He smiled and winked at her.

"No, that's okay. I'm fine. You guys have a long drive home."

Brynlei didn't want to be rude, but she wished her parents would leave her alone so she could get accustomed to her new surroundings. By the end of their lengthy drive to northern Michigan, their talk about the weather, the neighbor's overgrown shrubs, and suggestions for ways to make new friends had begun to suffocate her.

"We should probably start heading back before Derek burns the house down."

Derek opted to skip out on the long drive to nowhere. He remained in Franklin Corners playing video games with one of his buddies. As was the rule with older brothers, Derek knew exactly how to get under Brynlei's skin. "It's an art form, really," he liked to say about his ability to drive her up the wall. Yet she knew another side of Derek, too. The one that cared deeply for others, the one that made a point to leave money in the tip cup at Dairy Queen, even when no one was looking. The one who caught up to her as she burst out of Franklin Corners High, her face burning with humiliation from the rumors that Colton Smith had started. Derek's arms had held her together, preventing her from collapsing into a million pieces in the middle of the asphalt parking lot, as he recited all the reasons why Colton Smith was the biggest loser ever to walk the planet. She'd miss her brother when he left for Ann Arbor in the fall. If it weren't for Derek, Brynlei would be one hundred percent positive she was adopted.

"You can use the phone in the office to call us whenever you want," her mom said. Page eight of the brochure had warned about the lack of cell phone reception in Foxwoode's remote location. "Be sure to call us at least once a week to check in."

"I know, Mom. I'll be fine. I'm surrounded by horses, remember?"

"At least all this time apart will be good practice for college." Her mom squeezed her so tightly that Brynlei worried her ribs might crack.

"We'll miss you, Bryn." Her dad enveloped her in a bear hug. "Don't fall on your head."

"Thanks, Dad."

"We'll be back for your horse show," her mom promised.

Brynlei watched from the steps of Cabin 5 as her parents buckled themselves safely inside their SUV, waved to her out the windows, and disappeared back to their suburban life in a cloud of dust.

All at once, the reality of her situation hit her like a sucker punch to the gut. They were gone. She had been itching to get rid of them, but now that she stood all alone in her unfamiliar surroundings, she desperately wanted them to come back. She felt like an unsuspecting two year-old whose parents had just dropped her at daycare for the first time. She wasn't going to cry. Brynlei's face grew hot and tears welled up in her eyes. She took a deep breath in through her nose and exhaled through her mouth, just as the psychologist had taught her. She looked around. The sun illuminated her pale skin like a spotlight, alerting everyone of her solitary status.

A group of girls already in their bathing suits walked easily down the dirt pathway toward the lake. One of them laughed loudly and tried to steal the other girl's towel. In the other direction, dozens of horses grazed in rolling pastures framed by white fences. Brynlei breathed in the sweet scent of pine, grass, hay, and dandelions. A bee buzzed past her ear like an oncoming train. She shooed it away and walked toward the horses.

* * * *

Beyond the white fence that lined the pasture, horses grazed in a rolling meadow surrounded by a lush forest. The scenery appeared too perfect to be real. She couldn't believe she was really here. It had been her dream to attend Foxwoode since she was ten years old. Now, six years later, she had finally made it.

Her parents had thought her love of horses was a phase that she would outgrow, like playing Barbies or dressing up like princesses. "Foxwoode is for older girls," they told her when she was twelve. It was true; Foxwoode was for girls fourteen to eighteen only. However, much to her parents' dismay, Brynlei only grew more obsessed with riding the older she got, and she was good at it.

"You have natural talent," her riding instructor, Terri, told her after the first time she saw Brynlei jump a course. "I'm sure you've heard that before."

"I don't know," Brynlei replied, looking at the ground and smiling.

The truth was, no one had ever actually said those words to her, but she'd always known she had a special connection with the horses she rode. She could feel their next step before they took it. She could see the tricky distances before jumps that others missed. She instinctively knew when to pull back and collect or to let the horse lengthen and do its thing. These were skills that could rarely be taught.

"Foxwoode is expensive," her mom told her when she turned fourteen. "If you go, you won't be able to take riding lessons for the rest of the year."

Brynlei did not qualify for Foxwoode's scholarship opportunity because her parents did not suffer from Foxwoode's definition of financial hardship.

"I guess I make too much money." Her dad smiled and shrugged. "No one's ever told me that before." He winked at Brynlei's mom.

In any case, Brynlei chose the riding lessons over attending Foxwoode. She finagled opportunities to participate in a few horse shows, too. Blue ribbons adorned her bedroom walls.

When she turned fifteen, she chose the riding lessons again. After all, she couldn't go the whole year without riding. That was like giving someone the choice between an all-expenses-paid vacation to Hawaii or air to breathe. She had to choose the air.

On her sixteenth birthday, her parents surprised her—not with a car like some of her friends had recently received, but with a three-week summer session at Foxwoode Riding Academy. No strings attached. She knew the gift cost almost as much as a car. She leaped up and screamed, bouncing up and down as if their hardwood floor had transformed into a trampoline. Her tears flowed freely.

"Thank you! Thank you!" She'd sobbed and hugged her parents.

"Don't fall on your head," her dad said.

Brynlei wanted to reach out and pet some of the grazing horses and gaze into their knowing eyes, but an electrified wire ran along the inside panel of the fence. It was obviously intended to keep the horses in and the people out. She wasn't one to break the rules, especially on her first day at Foxwoode. She would have to be content to view the horses from a distance until tomorrow.

Page three of the Foxwoode brochure stated each girl who didn't bring her own horse would be assigned an appropriate horse to ride during her three-week stay. Which horse would be hers? They all looked so beautiful. She really couldn't go wrong.

Foxwoode's owners, Tom and Debbie Olson, spent their winters in Wellington, Florida, finding show horses to buy and bring back to Foxwoode for their students to ride and, sometimes, buy. Most of Foxwoode's horses were offered for sale at the end of the summer. That wouldn't be an option for Brynlei. Her parents had made it clear there was no room in their budget for a horse. Yet sometimes she let herself dream. She continued walking along the fence line to the main barn. She paused and peeked through the barn door before stepping into the first aisle. It took a second for her eyes to adjust to the darkness, but the familiar musty scent of hay and leather embraced her. The clip-clopping of hooves on cement echoed through the barn.

"Back up, Bentley," a high-pitched voice said from the next aisle. "He's such a brat."

"He's doin' good," a man's gruff voice said. "Bentley's in stall nine."

Brynlei peeked around the corner. A gorgeous gray thoroughbred still wearing his shipping boots was being led down the aisle by a tall blonde in a bright pink polo shirt. Her cut-off jean shorts gave way to impossibly long, tan legs. Brynlei instantly disliked the girl. She was always quick to judge people, but her instincts were usually right. A shiny black Hummer idled at the end of the aisle beside a deluxe four-stall horse trailer. The fumes choked Brynlei. A burly man in dirty jeans and leather work boots slid open a stall door. The box stall was almost as big as her bedroom at home.

"Alyssa, honey, do you need help?" A woman who looked like a slightly older version of the tall blonde and whose voice was almost as piercing spoke.

"Obviously, Mom. Take off his shipping boots. He doesn't like them," the girl ordered. Brynlei envisioned her own mom slapping her across the face if she ever talked to her that way.

"We need some hay in here," the girl barked at the man.

"Be right back," the man answered in a slow steady voice. Despite his enormous stature, he seemed like someone who was used to being ordered around.

The man walked down the aisle toward Brynlei and nodded at her without any change of expression. A black barn cat darted out in front of him and tried to weave itself in between the man's ankles. He picked up the cat and placed it gently on a hay bale.

"Hi," Brynlei squeaked out, sounding lame. Why hadn't she just nodded back?

She ran her hand over the cat's smooth, black coat and slipped over to the next aisle to look at the horses. Most were out in the pasture, but a few privately-owned horses were getting acclimated to their new spacious stalls. A sleek bay mare stared at her through the metal bars of her stall and calmly munched hay. Brynlei tried to tune out the constant whining of Alyssa and her mom from the next aisle.

"Did you see that blue-haired freak in our cabin?" Alyssa's voice pierced Brynlei's ears again.

"OMG! What's her deal, anyway?" Another girl laughed loudly. "She totally doesn't belong here."

Brynlei stood motionless, not wanting them to discover she was eavesdropping on their conversation. She didn't know who they were talking about. Brynlei hadn't seen anyone with blue hair.

"She's probably one of those scholarship people. Did you see her riding boots? They're not even real leather."

"That's sad." More laughter.

"Bentley had a better stall last year," Alyssa complained.

Brynlei inhaled sharply. The girls' shrill voices sounded like cats fighting. It would be quieter back in the cabin. As she walked past the Hummer, a man in a button-down shirt and sunglasses sat inside staring at his cell phone, cursing its poor reception. Alyssa's mom tried to get his attention by knocking on the window, but he waved her off. Brynlei realized her dad was right about one thing—the apple doesn't fall far from the tree.

Chapter Three

The wooden screen door of Cabin 5 slammed behind Brynlei, announcing her arrival.

"Hey," said a girl with a mess of blue hair and a nose ring. She sat on a pile of sheets in the bed directly above Brynlei's. "It's a bitch to make bunk beds. I'm Anna."

"Hi. I'm Brynlei." Her lack of coolness permeated the cabin. Hopefully, Anna wouldn't notice. She knew girls like Anna at her school, but never attempted to hang around with them. Girls like Anna intimidated her. Brynlei was more comfortable following the rules. She avoided drawing attention to herself at all costs, unless it was related to her riding.

Brynlei's parents would flip out at the sight of blue hair and a nose ring. They almost didn't let her get her ears pierced last year. She would never peg someone like Anna as an accomplished English rider. The sport was notoriously conservative in dress and style, especially at the level required to attend Foxwoode. She wondered if Anna removed her nose ring for horse shows. The blue hair could be hidden under her helmet, but the judges definitely wouldn't like the nose ring. Yet, she admired something about Anna's strong presence. Her appearance sent a clear message to the masses, like a giant middle finger.

Anna continued fumbling with her sheets. Brynlei guessed Anna's mom hadn't stuck around to make hospital corners for her.

"Do you need some help?" Brynlei said. "I mean, with the sheets?" She was overly aware of her voice. She wanted Anna to like her. Anna seemed like someone she'd want on her side.

"No. I'm good," Anna said. "Can you hand me my duffel bag,

though?"

Brynlei reached around the foot of the bunk bed and grabbed the black, half-zipped duffel off the hardwood floor. The bag was bursting at the seams, the thin threads of stitching barely holding the contents together. She tried to pass it up to Anna, but the awkward weight of the bag caused it to flip upside down. Brynlei ducked as a raggedy, pink teddy bear fell out of the bag and landed beside her on the floor.

"Crap," Anna said. She hung over the side of the bunk bed so far that Brynlei worried she might fall on the floor too.

"Sorry. The bag slipped."

Brynlei grabbed the bear and held it out to Anna. Anna's face turned red as she grabbed the bear and stuffed it under the messy sheets. "It's my sister's." Anna averted her eyes from Brynlei.

"I won't tell," Brynlei said. "It's no big deal anyway." It probably was a big deal to Anna, though. It would destroy her bad girl image if people knew that she slept with a pink teddy bear.

"I have a teddy bear at home too," Brynlei lied.

"I owe you one." Anna winked a charcoal-lined eye at Brynlei, as she buried the teddy bear under her pile of sheets.

Brynlei sensed there was more to Anna than met the eye. Anna emanated a calming energy from beneath the blue hair and nose ring. Brynlei pegged her as an old soul, someone who was highly evolved from her many past lives. Brynlei spent more time than she liked to admit thinking about past lives. Even before she'd been diagnosed as a "highly sensitive person" by the psychologist, she was fascinated by the idea that she had lived before and might live again.

A three-year-old boy she'd seen on TV a few years earlier had convinced her that past lives were real. The boy had been obsessed with planes. He only played with planes. He drew planes, mostly from the WW II era, and signed all his pictures "James 3." He talked about planes. He even dreamed about planes. In fact, the boy suffered a recurring nightmare of being trapped inside a burning plane.

Every day, he reported obscure details of a World War II air battle over Iwo Jima. After doing some research, his parents discovered that everything their son had been telling them had actually happened. A pilot named James M. Hudson, Jr. was shot down and killed during a little-known battle over Iwo Jima. The boy had correctly told his parents the name of the ship the plane took off from, the model of the plane, the fact that this model of plane often got flat tires from rough landings, the exact location the plane was struck by a Japanese missile, and even the name of the co-pilot on the flight.

The boy's parents were highly educated professionals who didn't need to make money off a sensational story. They insisted that their son had no way of knowing any of the information, that they had never spoken to him about World War II or let him watch any TV shows on the subject. The only explanation was that the boy had actually been that pilot in his past life. Because he was so young, he could still remember the traumatic events leading up to his previous death.

Brynlei had believed every word of the story. She was awestruck by the possibility that she could have lived past lives too. She began to read as much as possible on the subject and learned that she could have been a completely different person, or even an animal, in her past lives. She could have been male, female, Caucasian, African American, Asian, or Indian. The exterior package didn't matter. It was the soul that traveled on and carried knowledge from previous lives with it. The events of past lives could explain her irrational fears of seemingly harmless things and unquenchable passions for activities that others found boring. For Brynlei, this perfectly explained her fear of boats and her love of horses.

Sometimes she tried to envision who she'd be in her next life. She pictured a tall, elegant woman with wavy blond hair and golden skin. She'd be sophisticated, fashionable, and interesting. She'd be invited to garden parties and charity dinners, words easily flowing from her mouth, always knowing what to say. People would flock to her, laughing at her jokes or nodding along with her stories. She might live in California or Australia. Maybe she'd even be a movie star. Of course, her love for horses would travel with her. Brynlei knew that part for sure.

Rebecca's mom had once called Brynlei an old soul. Brynlei couldn't help feeling she understood more about life than most other people her age, or even many who were older. Anyway, she and Anna probably had that in common. Not to mention their synthetic leather riding boots. They both had the same pair lined up against the wall of Cabin 5. She instantly felt a kinship with Anna and hoped they could be friends. Now that Rebecca wasn't around, she needed a friend more than ever.

Brynlei found Anna surprisingly easy to talk to, mostly because she did all the talking. She twirled a section of her hair with her finger as she spoke, exposing the deep black roots under the shock of blue. Anna lived in Rochester Hills and had an older sister who would be a sophomore at the University of Vermont. Her mom ran a small art studio. Anna had been riding since she was seven. She'd owned her own horse, named Gemini, for three years. They were on track to compete on a national level.

"This is just between you and me." Anna's kohl-rimmed eyes bore into Brynlei.

"Yeah. I mean, of course."

"I dreamed of going to the Maclay with Gemini," Anna said, her eyes glassy. "Then the shit hit the fan with my dad's company."

It turned out Anna's dad's "company" was Chrysler. He had been one of Chrysler's top executives when there had been a recall that affected millions of cars. Class action lawsuits alleged that Chrysler had known about the defect, but not informed anyone. Anna's dad took the fall.

"I had to sell Gemini. My dad lost his job and my parents said they couldn't afford to pay for my horse." Anna stared at the floor as she picked at the remnants of her black nail polish.

"Sounds familiar," Brynlei said, trying to make connections with Anna anywhere she could.

"It sucked. I almost quit riding."

After being hung out to dry by Chrysler, Anna's dad had a mid-life crisis. Anna added quotation marks with her fingers as she said the words. Her parents had separated for eight months. Anna's mom took her dad back three months ago and they were trying to work things out.

"My dad has his own consulting business now. They said I could come here this summer. It's supposed to be some kind of consolation prize for their separation and for selling Gemini. Also, it's the closest they can come to sending me to boarding school." Anna coughed out a laugh.

Just then, two petite girls, one slightly taller with a nest of curly red hair and the other with short brown hair cut into an angled bob, returned to the cabin. Despite their contrasting hairstyles, they looked like two pieces to the same puzzle. Their matching sunglasses were propped up on their heads at exactly the same angle, and they wore bikini tops with towels wrapped around their waists. Brynlei wanted to ask them if they shopped two-for-one specials, but she kept the thought to herself. In truth, she was jealous of how comfortable they were with their bodies. Even at an all-girls camp, she would never walk around in just a bikini top without feeling the judgmental eyes of everyone around her burning into her skin. She always wore a cover-up.

"Hey," the brown-haired girl said nonchalantly, as if they had known each other for years. They made their introductions. Julia with the brown hair and Kaitlyn with the red hair were friends from home. They lived in Grand Rapids. This was their second summer at Foxwoode.

"I mean, you're going to learn so much. Seriously, you'll love it," Kaitlyn assured Brynlei, her hair bouncing as she talked.

Then Julia, who talked out of the side of her mouth, made an inside joke about green bean casserole that no one understood except Kaitlyn. Kaitlyn flung her curls back and laughed. Brynlei wanted to laugh at a joke. She missed Rebecca.

A few minutes later, Alyssa, the girl from the barn, entered. Brynlei sucked in her breath and closed her eyes. It was going to be a long three weeks. Why hadn't she packed earplugs?

"Seriously, Top Rider? In my cabin?" Kaitlyn said, pointing at Alyssa. "She was Top Rider last year."

"Oh, that's great," Brynlei said, forcing her voice to be unnaturally high-pitched. Acting was not her strong suit.

"Alyssa is seriously awesome," Kaitlyn said. "Her horse, Bentley, is to die for."

Page eight of the Foxwoode brochure stated that, at the end of every session, Foxwoode awarded a Top Rider award to the girl who rose above the rest to demonstrate clear excellence in horsemanship and riding. The winner of the Top Rider award was invited back for the following summer, free of charge. Of course, every girl at Foxwoode wanted to win Top Rider and Brynlei was no exception. Yet she was horrified that someone like Alyssa was the winner. Now she wanted the award even more, if only to ensure that it did not go to Alyssa again.

A heavy-set blonde with eyes like mud-pies followed closely behind Alyssa. "I'm McKenzie," she said, to no one in particular. McKenzie appeared to be Alyssa's slightly slower and less-attractive twin.

"McKenzie and I board at the same barn in Chicago. We trailer our horses here every summer," Alyssa said.

"Bentley and Lilly," McKenzie added.

"You're new, right?" Alyssa said to Brynlei.

"Yeah. It's my first time here."

"Do you have a horse?" The way Alyssa asked the question seemed more like an accusation than a friendly inquiry.

"No. I mean, not my own. I leased a horse last year. Actually, it was a half-lease..." Brynlei's voice trailed off.

"What's up with your hair?" Alyssa said to Anna, apparently too bored with Brynlei's answer to pay attention. McKenzie looked at the floor and snickered.

"It's just my style. My name's Anna, by the way. I have some extra dye if you're game."

"Um, no thanks," Alyssa responded, with McKenzie still snickering in her shadow.

Anna rolled her eyes and continued reading as if nothing had happened. Brynlei didn't know how Anna could let Alyssa's insults roll off her back like that. Even before Brynlei found out she was a highly sensitive person, she knew she felt things more deeply than those around her did.

She did not have the thick skin that people always said was necessary to make it through life. She did not understand the invisible force field that others could erect around themselves. A wall that protected them from all of the horrific events that occurred every day. People could watch a tsunami devastate an entire country on the news and then go eat a hamburger for dinner, as if they didn't have a care in the world. Meanwhile, the haunting images from the newsreel stayed with Brynlei and begged her to help them.

A picture of a starving dog on the ASPCA commercial could send her into a deep depression for the whole day. It was as if she became the dog. She could feel its emotions, its innocence, its hunger, its desire to be loved. On some level, she'd always been conscious of her unique connection to animals. Ever since the night she'd watched the deer die, she had no doubt.

Brynlei's sensitivities went beyond animals. A negative remark by someone she barely knew could also send her reeling into her own mind.

"Nice dress," Aaron Martin had said to Brynlei the Monday she'd worn the turquoise dress to school.

She had bought it the day before with encouragement from her mother and the saleslady at Uptown Threads. They convinced her she needed to be more daring with her wardrobe.

"You can't wear blue jeans and sweaters every day," her mother had said, followed by a deep sigh.

"This style is very popular right now," the saleslady added.

In the end, they outnumbered her. The saleslady convinced her that the dress accentuated her curves in all the right places. Brynlei wasn't aware she had any curves, so that was a big selling point, but she did like the dress. It was different from anything else she owned. So she bought it.

However, on that Monday morning in geometry, she heard the thick sarcasm in Aaron Martin's voice. *Nice dress. Nice dress.*

Why did he say that? What was wrong with her dress? She repeated the scene over and over in her head. She couldn't focus on geometry or English or history, just the comment about the dress.

When she finally saw Rebecca in the hall, she spoke to her, "What's wrong with my dress?"

"Nothing. It's super cute," Rebecca said. "You should wear dresses more often."

She never wore a dress to school again.

Brynlei felt the energy of the world around her. The tangible vibrations of thoughts, of actions, of things that were about to happen, and of things that had already happened. She didn't see the energy in pictures. She couldn't see faces or numbers or letters, like the psychics on TV. It was more like tiny specks of light, like static electricity, that her body and mind absorbed. Sometimes the energy was bright and happy. Other times it was dark. A warning. She couldn't help but feel it. She didn't know how to ignore it.

"Are you going to start wearing tin foil on your head?" Rebecca said once when Brynlei described the feeling to her. "Because that would be embarrassing."

Rebecca didn't question Brynlei's sensitivities though. Rebecca believed her.

Months before the psychologist's diagnosis, Brynlei had known about Derek's car accident before it happened. It was Saturday morning and the girls were waking up in the matching twin beds in Brynlei's room.

"How late can you hang out today?" Rebecca asked.

"I should leave for my riding lesson by ten thirty," Brynlei said. "You can come with me if you want."

"I need to practice violin this afternoon. It's my only time to do it this weekend," Rebecca replied. "Besides, I'm terrified of horses."

"You must have been trampled by a herd of wild horses in your past life."

"That must have been what happened." Rebecca rolled her eyes. She was used to Brynlei conjecturing about her past lives.

"Do you feel weird today," Brynlei asked.

"I always feel weird."

"No. I mean, I feel a weird energy around me. Like I'm being crushed, but not really crushed, just the air is heavy, or something." Brynlei mustered the energy to prop herself up on the bed. Somehow, her body had taken on the weight of a thousand bricks.

"I have no idea what you're talking about," Rebecca said. "The air feels nice and light over here." Rebecca bounced up and down on the twin bed to make her point.

Brynlei tried to ignore the air that pressed in on her while she pulled on her clothes and splashed cold water on her face. The smell of pancakes, butter, and syrup wafted through the upstairs hallway and drew the two girls down to the kitchen where Brynlei's dad was manning the griddle. Derek sat at the kitchen table, devouring the pancakes on the plate in front of him. He gulped down a glass of orange juice.

"You should try chewing your food sometime," Rebecca said. She was Derek's honorary second little sister.

"You again," Derek said with a smirk. "Don't you have a family?"

"Here you go, girls." Brynlei's dad set down two plates of pancakes in front of them.

The dark energy closed in on Brynlei, surrounding her. Rebecca said something to her dad, but Brynlei couldn't register the words. It sounded like they were speaking in a foreign language. The air trapped Brynlei inside its invisible walls. Beads of sweat formed on her forehead. Her lungs filled with sand. She couldn't breathe. She ran to the bathroom and gagged, dry-heaving into the toilet.

"Bryn, what's wrong?" her dad said. "Do you have the flu?"

"No. Not the flu." She sat on cold tile of the bathroom floor breathing heavily. She looked straight at Derek. "Something bad is going to happen today."

An hour later, Derek was driving his Chevy Impala down a quiet, tree-lined road, rapping along to an Eminem song. He would have been five minutes early for varsity baseball practice at Franklin Corners High School, except for the pickup truck that ran the red light and barreled into the side of Derek's car, breaking Derek's right leg in three places. Later, as Brynlei and her parents visited Derek in his hospital room, they found out that the driver of the truck wasn't wearing his seatbelt. He had died on impact. They sat, speechless, the color draining from their collective faces as they absorbed the awful news before becoming overwhelmed with gratitude that somehow Derek had narrowly avoided the same fate.

Her parents and Derek had brushed off her premonition as a "weird coincidence." Brynlei knew it was more than that, and Rebecca had believed her.

Alyssa's shrill voice jolted Brynlei back to the present.

"Well, ladies, we're heading off to the boring introduction dinner. See you over there," Alyssa said, in a tone that indicated she couldn't care less whether she saw them there or not. Alyssa applied some lip-gloss and walked out the door with McKenzie following in her shadow. Kaitlyn and Julia trailed a few steps behind.

"You guys coming?" Julia said before she slipped out the door.

"Yeah," Brynlei said, getting up from her bunk. A cold sweat broke out all over her body. Walking into a mess hall full of people she didn't know was terrifying. She needed Rebecca.

Anna climbed down from the top bunk and walked toward the door next to her.

"Alyssa is a first-class bitch," Anna said under her breath.

Brynlei couldn't help smiling.

She forced herself to follow the mob of teenage girls toward the mess hall, as if she was one of a herd of cattle being led to slaughter. As she dragged along the dirt path, she breathed in deeply through her nose and out through her mouth, not wanting to cause a scene. These things were never as bad as she imagined. Still, she was relieved to have Anna next to her. At least she wouldn't be sitting alone.

Chapter Four

Walking through the doors of the mess hall was like arriving at a chuck wagon in Montana. Foxwoode's decorator seemed to have confused the English riding academy theme with a Western cowboy dude ranch theme. Brynlei liked it. It felt warm and homey, which was just what she needed. Large wooden beams crisscrossed the high ceiling. Rustic tables with benches instead of chairs were covered with red-and-white-checkered table clothes. A massive fireplace surrounded with stones adorned one wall, and good luck horse shoes hung from every available nook and cranny.

"Welcome. Welcome." A woman's voice boomed over a microphone. "Everyone go through the line, get your dinner, and find a place to sit."

"That's Debbie Olson," Anna said. "I met her earlier. She didn't like my hair." Her upper lip curled into a half-smile. Brynlei recognized Debbie from when she'd checked in at the office earlier.

Debbie and her husband, Tom, were in their fifties and the owners of Foxwoode. They were both imposing figures—tall, outspoken, and well-dressed. Their features were perfectly symmetrical, like plastic dolls. With Debbie's statuesque build and sculpted platinum hair and Tom's confident gaze, enormous stature, and million-dollar smile, they looked like they had grown up amongst the horsey set. The Olsons were known to be hands-on and sticklers for making sure everyone followed the rules. The tight structure of Foxwoode didn't bother Brynlei. She couldn't think of a rule she'd broken in her life, at least not on purpose.

"Looks like spaghetti night," Brynlei said, stating the obvious. She took a tray from the pile. "I hope they have a vegetarian option." She already knew they served "vegan alternatives" from page eleven of the Foxwoode brochure, but she was desperate to make conversation.

"Are you vegan?" Anna said, turning toward Brynlei.

"Yeah. I mean, I'm a vegetarian. I love my mom's cookies too much. I can't give up the eggs."

"It's not much harder," Anna said. "Just use an egg substitute."

Brynlei helped herself to a piece of garlic bread and a heap of green salad. Then she spooned marinara sauce over the pile of noodles on her plate and handed the ladle to Anna. Her stomach growled with hunger. She hadn't eaten anything since stopping at McDonald's with her parents several hours ago. The lemonade and McSalad that she only picked at were no longer cutting it.

There were already a few people sitting at every table. Brynlei saw Kaitlin and Julia sitting nearby. She headed toward them because she didn't know what else to do. Anna followed and slid onto the bench next to her.

"Seriously, it's like spaghetti night every other night here," Kaitlin said.

"The food's not bad though," Julia added. "You can always buy candy in the store."

Brynlei chewed her food faster than she intended. The marinara sauce was different from the one she made at home—less garlic, more onions—but it was decent. She was so hungry that anything probably would have tasted good.

Alyssa and McKenzie sat at the table in front of them. They were laughing with a group of girls. Brynlei didn't get it. She always tried to be nice to people. She was smart and funny. She was better-than-average looking, but making friends did not come easily to her. She did not want friends badly enough to act fake and snobby, like Alyssa. She'd rather be alone.

Anna nudged her. "Looks like our friend has a fan club."

Brynlei shook her head and smiled through clenched teeth.

"Hello, everyone," Debbie said into the microphone. "Welcome to Summer Session II at Foxwoode! For those of you who haven't met me, I'm Debbie Olson and this is my husband, Tom. We've been the owners of Foxwoode for the last eighteen years."

A scattered applause and a handful of cheers filled the silence.

"I trust you're all settled into your cabins and ready to ride."

More hoots and hollers rang out.

"Before we kick things off with a bonfire tonight, I'd like to introduce you to our staff and go over some rules. Feel free to keep eating while we talk."

Brynlei could have hugged Debbie. She chewed her food slower now that she didn't have to worry about making conversation.

"First, we have six top-notch riding instructors whom we're lucky to have with us for the summer. Each instructor is assigned to one cabin. They will check in on you at least three times a day and will make sure that lights are out at ten sharp every night. There is also a final bunk check at midnight. If you have any problems, you can find your instructors in their individual cabins located between the mess hall and the main barn. Please don't bother them on their off hours unless it is truly an emergency. Just to be clear, losing your bag of gummy bears does not constitute an emergency."

A smattering of laughter echoed through the high ceilings.

"So without further ado, Cabin 1, your instructor is Ashley Robbins."

Miss Ashley, as she wished to be called, stepped forward and talked about her experience riding and coaching the equestrian team at Western Michigan University. She'd led her team to the nationals two years in a row after attending Foxwoode for three summers as a teen. "I'm excited to be back at Foxwoode as an instructor," Miss Ashley said before pumping her fist in the air and bounding back to her seat.

One by one, the instructors for each cabin stepped forward and recited their impressive qualifications. Brynlei sat on the edge of the bench waiting for the Cabin 5 instructor to step forward.

Finally, a woman who appeared to be in her late twenties stood up. Her short, spiked-up black hair accentuated her pale skin and blue eyes.

"I'm Jill Redmond. Please call me Miss Jill," she said into the microphone. "I'll be with Cabin 5."

Miss Jill's British accent immediately enthralled Brynlei. Miss Jill ran through her credentials. She grew up outside of London, where she owned her first pony at the age of three. She'd competed in England's top levels of hunters and equitation as a teenager. She went on to study equine management at the University of Greenwich. As if that wasn't enough, she'd spent a summer in Ireland studying horse training using natural horsemanship methods.

"I've always wanted to travel to the States," Miss Jill continued. "So when Foxwoode called me with this opportunity, I took it. I look forward to getting to know all of you over the next three weeks."

"Sweet accent," Anna said.

"Now," Debbie boomed, "just a few more introductions. We have four people on our kitchen staff. They are back for their fifth year to cook all of this wonderful food for us. Maggie, Dean, Lynn, and Martin."

The four cooks poked their heads out of the kitchen and waved quickly, seemingly embarrassed by their moment of glory.

There was more applause, although this time it was less energetic.

Debbie continued. "We have one full-time barn hand you'll see working hard around the barn every day. Bruce Haslow. Bruce has been our loyal employee for ten years now."

Bruce stood halfway up and nodded briefly to the crowd of girls. Brynlei immediately recognized him as the large man in the barn from earlier in the day. Did Bruce hate his job? He must, after getting ordered around by girls like Alyssa.

"Last, but not least, I'd like to introduce last year's recipient of Foxwoode's Top Rider award, Alyssa Smithson."

Alyssa stood up and waved, as the girls around her cheered.

"Alyssa, we're so glad you and Bentley came back to join us again. We know you'll be a great mentor to the other girls."

Mentor? She and Anna looked at each other and laughed in spite of themselves.

"If you need to find me or Mr. Olson for any reason," Debbie continued, "we live in the house on the hill and we're in the office daily. Be sure to follow all the rules in the handbook that we mailed to you and you shouldn't have any problems here. Happy riding. Have fun at the bonfire tonight."

* * * *

On the beach, daylight dwindled behind the trees and created an eerie orange glow. The moon hung low and faded in the sky, the stars not yet visible. Flames lashed out from the crackling fire and contrasted with the glassy, silver water of the lake lapping up on the beach. Across the lake, the dense wall of the forest steadily darkened from gray to black.

Brynlei pulled the sleeves of her blue hooded sweatshirt down over her hands and crossed her arms. Nights in Northern Michigan could be chilly, even in July, and tonight was no exception. She and Anna sat on the second row of logs back from the bonfire, occasional waves of heat from the fire drifting over them.

Miss Ashley and Miss Julia passed out sticks and marshmallows to the girls sitting around the fire. Miss Jill stood farther away with a bag full of graham cracker boxes and Hershey's chocolate bars.

Brynlei threaded two marshmallows on her stick and held it out carefully over the fire. The many bonfires at her aunt and uncle's cottage had taught her how to roast the marshmallows to a perfect golden brown. Rebecca, on the other hand, always stuck her marshmallows straight into the fire, watched them go up in flames, and then blew them out. "Perfect!" she would announce with delight, as white goo oozed out of the holes in the crispy black shell. Brynlei noticed Anna used the same fiery technique as Rebecca for roasting her marshmallows.

All around, girls chattered. They talked about their favorite horses at Foxwoode and at home. They talked about horse shows they'd competed in earlier in the summer and ones they would travel to in August and September. They talked about boyfriends and boys they wanted to be their boyfriends. Brynlei mostly listened, only chiming in to mention, Rosie, the horse she half-leased for most of last year, and the classes they entered at Stoneywood Farms in June. She was not one to brag. If she were, she would have mentioned that she and Rosie had won champion of their division at Stoneywood. Brynlei preferred to fly under the radar. A dark horse, someone once called her. Whenever she won, nobody saw it coming.

"Does anyone have a good ghost story?" Miss Jill requested in her crisp British accent. It was almost nine now and the sky grew darker by the minute.

"I do," one of the younger girls yelled. "It's really spooky."

Brynlei licked gooey marshmallows from her fingers, as the girl told a story of a babysitter who, after putting the kids to bed, heard strange noises coming from upstairs. The babysitter's phone rang. When she answered, a man asked, "Have you checked on the children?" The babysitter ignored the call the first time, but the man kept calling back and asking the same creepy question. The babysitter finally called the police and convinced them to trace the call. The police informed the babysitter the call was coming from inside the house. The babysitter ran upstairs and found that all of the children had been decapitated. Their heads hung in a neat row on hooks in the upstairs hallway.

The crowd screamed and laughed. Someone complained that the girl got the story wrong and proceeded to tell a slightly different version, in which the parents came home and found the kids' and the babysitter's heads on hooks in the downstairs hallway.

Another girl told a story about a serial killer loose at a summer camp, which sounded a lot like the movie *Friday the 13th*.

"I have a ghost story," Alyssa's high-pitched voice called from the back row.

"This should be good," Anna muttered under her breath.

"It's scary because it's true," Alyssa continued. "It happened here. At Foxwoode."

With the exception of the crackling fire and a few crickets chirping in the distance, there was complete silence. Everyone turned to look at Alyssa.

"It happened just four years ago," Alyssa said. "Caroline Watson was fifteen and from a small town somewhere near Lansing. It was her first summer at Foxwoode. She was young, but she was a kickass horse trainer and one of the best riders ever to come through Foxwoode. She was also gorgeous. Tall and model thin with perfect skin, long, shiny black hair, and bright green eyes, Caroline turned heads. Some of the other girls didn't like that. They were jealous of her riding and her looks."

"Is that how you feel, Alyssa?" someone said with a hint of sarcasm.

"Every day." Alyssa flashed her perfect smile, and a few of the girls laughed. She clearly enjoyed being the center of attention.

"Anyway, two weeks into Caroline's three-week session, she was the favorite for the Top Rider award. Everyone knew she would get it.

One afternoon, Caroline took a trail ride on the young horse she was helping to train. Then, she screwed up big time. She went on the trail ride by herself and wasn't wearing her helmet. She didn't tell anyone she was leaving or where she was going. No one even realized she was missing until her horse came back that night, his saddle hanging to the side. He was covered in mud."

Brynlei had never heard of a horse returning from a trail ride without its rider. She dug her toes into the sand and leaned forward, not wanting to miss a word.

"The search for Caroline began immediately. Search teams canvassed the forest for three miles in every direction. The second day of the search, someone discovered one of Caroline's paddock boots floating in Big Rapids River about a mile and half east of here. They found some of her blood and hair on a jagged rock near the river's edge. They said she must have lost control of her horse, fallen off, hit her head, and drowned in the river. Or died somewhere out in the woods. She was presumed dead. To this day, her body has never been found."

The girls listened in silence. Only the lapping waves and chirping crickets hummed in the background.

"Some believe her death was an accident. Others believe it was something more sinister. Perhaps she was murdered by some of the girls who were jealous of her. Some people suspect the creepy barn hand, Bruce, who still lurks around our cabins."

Some nervous laughter escaped from the mouths of a few.

Alyssa lowered her voice. "They say Caroline's spirit never left Foxwoode. They say she will never rest in peace until her body is found and given a proper burial. Over the years, people have seen her ghost in the woods and in the barn. She is there one moment and gone the next. Sometimes items go mysteriously missing from the cabins. Two summers ago, one girl woke up in the middle of the night and saw a ghost with long black hair and glowing green eyes standing over her bed. She closed her eyes and tried to scream, but no sound would come out. When she opened her eyes again, the ghost was gone."

As much as Brynlei disliked Alyssa, she had to hand it to her. Alyssa could tell one heck of a creepy story.

"So, if you awake to a thump in the night or you're on a trail ride and suddenly feel uneasy, you know that the ghost of Caroline Watson is there. She's in your cabin. She's hiding behind the trees. She is always watching you."

"BOO!" someone yelled. Everyone jumped and screamed, and then laughed.

"Is that really a true story, Alyssa?" asked the girl who had told the babysitter story earlier.

"The part about Caroline disappearing on a trail ride is true," Alyssa said. "Everyone knows about that. The stuff about the ghost is a load of crap. People keep adding to the story every summer."

"Okay, girls. That's enough talk about Caroline Watson. It was a tragic event. The Olsons don't need us spreading rumors," Miss Jill said. "It's after nine thirty. We all need to get back to our cabins."

Some of the girls filled buckets of water to put out the fire, but Brynlei shuffled her feet through the sand toward the path. She couldn't wait to climb into her tightly made bed and sleep away the stress of the day. She gazed out at the glassy black lake, mesmerized by the rhythmic sound of lapping waves. Something caught her eye in the woods beyond the lake. A hint of movement, almost imperceptible, except for the thousand pin pricks of static electricity surging through her body. She froze. She could feel a presence. Brynlei squinted into the darkness, searching for the shadowy figure she thought she'd glimpsed. Then, as quickly as it had appeared, it was gone.

* * * *

Sleep did not come easily to Brynlei that night. Long after lights out at ten and long after the other girls stopped whispering and giggling, Brynlei lay awake in her bunk and stared through the darkness at the wooden slats above her. When Miss Jill popped her head in the door for the midnight bunk check, Brynlei closed her eyes and pretended to be asleep. Anna breathed heavily in the top bunk. Someone turned over in their sleep on the other side of the room. Crickets chirped relentlessly outside the screen window.

Brynlei's thoughts were like a leaky faucet she couldn't turn off. Which horse would be assigned to her tomorrow? Would she be able to ride at the same level as the other girls? Despite memorizing the pages of the Foxwoode brochure, she had no idea what to expect.

So, what had she seen across the lake? Was it a person? The same person she'd glimpsed by the shed on the service road? Could the ghost story about Caroline Watson be true? No, that was crazy. The stress of her new surroundings was making her lose her mind.

Brynlei yearned for the familiarity of home—the smell of her mom's freshly-baked butterscotch cookies, the sound of Maverick's nails clicking across the hardwood floors, and the predictability of her dad's dumb jokes. If only she could talk to Rebecca. She needed to tell her about Alyssa, Anna, and Miss Jill, and the weird feeling she'd had after the bonfire. Rebecca would be fast asleep by now. Not a worry in the world kept Rebecca awake.

* * * *

In ninth grade, Rebecca had been the first to have a real boyfriend. Brynlei knew all about Rebecca's crush on Jason Bartly. Rebecca talked endlessly about Jason's dreamy blue eyes, cute crooked smile, and the funny jokes he cracked in biology. Her secret was safe with Brynlei. After all, Rebecca was holding inside information about Brynlei's crush on Colton Smith. Brynlei's infatuation with Colton didn't add up for Rebecca.

"You like a skater boy?" she said, shaking her head. "Can you imagine your dates? He'd be like, 'Dude, watch my next trick.' Then he'd crash into a wall, break his arm, and you'd nurse him back to health in the emergency room."

"Sounds good to me," Brynlei responded. Then they both laughed. For Brynlei, it was the kind of laugh that came from her gut. The kind of laugh that could make milk squirt out her nose.

Anyway, she didn't think Rebecca and Jason would actually become an item, and she really didn't think that they would stay together for as long as they had. She'd never tell Rebecca this, but she thought popular and athletic Jason was a strange match for Rebecca. Then one Wednesday evening in the fall of their freshman year, Rebecca called Brynlei.

"You'll never guess what just happened. Jason called me. I'm freaking out."

Brynlei was happy for her friend, but she couldn't deny the pang of jealousy that tore through her gut. "Tell me everything," she ordered, swallowing back the sour taste in her mouth.

Rebecca recounted the awkward conversation, the invitation to see a movie on Saturday night, the overly-eager acceptance. Brynlei clung to every word and lived vicariously through her friend.

Later, Brynlei would have her turn with Colton, but her experience wouldn't go so smoothly. Rebecca stuck by her, though. Rebecca had never believed the rumors Colton started—the ones that multiplied exponentially throughout Franklin Corners High School. They always had each other's backs. Even with Jason popping his head into the middle of the picture, their friendship was unsinkable. They had known each other too long and laughed too many times to have it any other way.

The wooded slats above Brynlei shifted slightly as Anna rolled over in her sleep. Brynlei wondered if Caroline Watson had trouble sleeping her first night at Foxwoode. Had Caroline missed her home too? Did she ever imagine that she would never see her family and friends again? What really happened to her? Was it an accident or murder? Who or what had Brynlei seen today? It was probably her imagination running away with her. The thoughts spun like a never-ending cyclone through her head. It wasn't until two in the morning that the winds began to die and she drifted off to sleep.

Chapter Five

Brynlei stood shoulder to shoulder with the other five girls in her cabin, the advanced sixteen-and-older riders, or the Flying Foxes, as they'd be referred to henceforth. During breakfast, Miss Jill informed them their cabin would also be their riding group and, not surprisingly, Miss Jill was their instructor.

The four other cabins were also formed into groups based on age and riding level, either intermediate or advanced. There were no beginner riders at Foxwoode. The formation of the riding groups formed a social hierarchy of sorts. The advanced riders were the envy of the intermediate riders. The advanced riders, Brynlei included, couldn't help but walk with their shoulders stretched a little taller.

The Flying Foxes stood fidgeting outside the main barn, awaiting their horse assignments. Of course, Alyssa and McKenzie already knew they would be riding their own horses, but they waited with the others. The air pulsed with a nervous energy. Anna picked at a speck of polish on her pinkie nail. Brynlei waited next to Anna, their matching synthetic leather boots reflecting the sun. Alyssa stared at their boots and elbowed McKenzie, her mouth curling into a vicious smile.

Foxwoode's placement process began several months earlier. Each girl was required to submit a recommendation and evaluation from her riding instructor at home. Brynlei remembered clearly the night she showed the forms to Terri.

She had arrived extra-early to her Wednesday night riding lesson and walked over to Terri, who was teaching a beginner jumping lesson in the indoor arena. Brynlei couldn't stop her hand from shaking as she

36

held out the papers to Terri.

"Foxwoode," Terri said, reading the application. "I always wanted to go there. My parents wouldn't pay for it." She forced a laugh.

The air deflated from Brynlei, as if her parents' willingness to pay for her summer at Foxwoode had somehow caused Terri's parents not to have the money. She stood in front of Terri, not knowing what to say.

"No, this is great," Terri said, suddenly trying to lighten the mood. "You are well-qualified, that's for sure."

She spent the rest of the evening and most of the next day obsessing over what Terri would write about her on the application. When she arrived at the barn on Thursday, Terri handed the paperwork back to her. The evaluation was neatly filled out. The recommendation ran over onto the back of the page.

"I had a lot of good things to say about you," Terri said.

"Thank you," Brynlei said, and meant it.

Brynlei's teachers, including her riding instructors, had always sung her praises. She was the ideal student. She followed instructions, turned in her homework on time, and never caused problems. She was either on time, or five minutes early for her classes and riding lessons. She was smart—her memory, like a steel vault. Brynlei presumed she'd inherited a strain of perfectionism from her mom. That's why she'd never be happy with an A minus or a second place ribbon.

As soon as Brynlei was sheltered by the privacy of her car, her eyes poured over the evaluation. She didn't waste any time reading the evaluation's questions, which she had already memorized, just Terri's answers.

"Brynlei's equitation on the flat is textbook perfect. Her position over fences has improved dramatically in the last year... she is able to adjust her riding to allow her horse to show off his movement... Brynlei does not own her own horse. I am consistently impressed with her riding and her ability to adapt to different horses."

She couldn't drink in the words fast enough. Her eyes kept leaping ahead of her.

"Brynlei has not trained a truly green horse, although I believe she has the ability to do this with some guidance. She is a patient rider...

"Brynlei understands horse behavior and relates easily to the horses… She typically jumps 2'9" or 3', although she can jump 3'6" on the right horse…

"At shows, Brynlei consistently placed at the top of the children's hunter and equitation classes last year. She has the ability to progress further in her showing career. Brynlei always challenges herself to improve in every area of her riding."

The last question, which Brynlei knew was the most important one: "Do you recommend this student to Foxwoode?" awaited her.

"Brynlei is an ideal candidate for Foxwoode. She is a hard worker and a naturally talented rider and horsewoman. Any riding school would be lucky to have her."

Brynlei read the evaluation again and again. She couldn't stop herself from smiling. Terri rarely gave Brynlei compliments when she rode. Terri was not one to sugarcoat things or say things that weren't true. If Terri said nothing while Brynlei rode, that meant she was doing well. The words on the paper validated all of her hard work. At that moment, Brynlei knew the "i"s were dotted and the "t"s were crossed. She was going to Foxwoode.

She turned the key in the ignition and turned up the volume on her radio. An overplayed Katy Perry song boomed through the speakers, but Brynlei didn't care. She had belted out the words and driven home. Happy.

* * * *

"Once you all have your horse assignments, you may go find your horse and begin tacking up. Brushes and tack are in the lockers across from the stalls," Miss Jill said. "We'll be riding in Ring A, beginning at nine sharp. Now, let's begin, shall we? Kaitlyn, you'll be with Daisey." Katilyn squealed with delight. "Julia, you'll have Devon."

"Yes," Julia whispered out of the side of her mouth.

"Anna, you'll be paired with Rebel," Miss Jill said. "And, Brynlei, you'll be riding Jett." She didn't know which horse Jett was, but she liked the name. To be honest, she would have been happy to ride any of the horses at Foxwoode.

The Flying Foxes skittered down the barn aisle, searching for their horses like starving pirates on the brink of discovering a valuable treasure. From the moment Brynlei saw Jett, she was smitten. He was a large horse, about sixteen hands, with kind brown eyes that seemed to recognize her instantly. His deep black coat was stunning. It was obvious how he got his name.

She slid open the stall door and rubbed his neck and forehead. Jett's warm breath found her hand as he searched for a treat. Brynlei slipped the nylon halter that hung on the front of the stall over Jett's nose. Jett munched hay and looked at her while she clipped the lead rope to the ring on the bottom of the halter and carefully led Jett to one of the many grooming stalls.

Miss Jill made the rounds, giving each girl important information about her horse. When she reached Brynlei, she stopped, "How are you getting on with Jett?" Her British accent was charming. Rebecca would have a field day.

"Great," Brynlei said. "I love him." It only took her a few seconds to fall in love with a horse.

"He's a good boy. Very willing. He's a young one though, maybe six. He'll need you for guidance." Miss Jill winked at her. "Make sure he wears a martingale, a wither pad, and front boots."

Brynlei picked out Jett's hooves and then curried his already shiny coat. As she brushed, she peeked around the corner and saw Anna grooming a muscular chestnut horse with a gleaming white blaze.

"Rebel will give you a run for your money," Miss Jill told Anna. "He'll try to run out on jumps occasionally. You can handle him though."

"I'm not worried," Anna said, standing tall. "He reminds me of the horse I ride at home."

After Brynlei finished grooming Jett, she laid the white saddle pad emblazoned with the word "FOXWOODE" on his back. She set the wither pad on top of it. She carefully draped the martingale around Jett's neck. Next came the saddle. She buckled the girth on the right side first, slid it through the martingale, and buckled it, not too tightly, on the other side. She found Jett's boots in the locker and wrapped them around each of his front legs, pulling the Velcro straps snuggly to keep them in place.

She picked up her helmet next, pulled her hair back into a hairnet, and twisted it all up on top of her head. Brynlei slid the helmet over her head and clicked the strap snuggly under her chin. Then she unclipped Jett from his halter and slid the bridal over his head. He accepted the bit easily. She buckled the noseband and chinstrap on the bridle, pulled on her riding gloves, and grabbed a crop from the locker. She was ready to ride.

* * * *

Out in Ring A, the morning sun peeked over the tree line in the distance. Dust floated and glistened in the air above the sandy ring. Brynlei tightened Jett's girth and swung her leg over the saddle. She sat atop Jett and adjusted her stirrups. She tried to avoid leather whenever possible, which was difficult as a rider. She didn't own her own saddle yet, so she used the one provided by Foxwoode—a Pessoa close contact saddle that was likely made out of calf skin. She was used to making exceptions for leather, especially when she didn't have a choice. This saddle was hers for the next three weeks and she'd take care of it. She needed the stirrups to be just the right length, hitting her anklebone if she let her legs hang down.

The other girls led their horses to the mounting blocks and climbed up into their saddles, one by one. The Flying Foxes, perfectly turned out in their tan breeches, tall boots, black helmets, polo shirts, and matching "Foxwoode" saddle pads, had an air of royalty about them. This wasn't your run-of-the-mill horse camp.

Miss Jill dragged four ground poles into a row on the quarter line several feet apart from each other as the riders warmed up.

"Everyone track left and pick up your posting trot." Miss Jill's voice suddenly assumed the tone of an army drill sergeant.

Brynlei stretched tall, sunk down into her heels, and squeezed her calves around Jett. He trotted forward. In contrast to Rosie's short, choppy trot, Jett's trot was big and bouncy. She posted, rising and falling with each step, getting used to her new horse's gait.

Every few minutes, Miss Jill called out a new order. "Everyone find a place to circle." Then, "Everyone turn down the quarter line and trot the ground poles." She critiqued the riders as they passed her. "Keep stretching up tall, McKenzie. Raise your right hand slightly, Anna. Look where you want to go, Kaitlin. Get him even more on the bit, Brynlei."

Brynlei immediately made the adjustment, pulling lightly on alternating reins so that Jett lowered his head as she pushed him forward with her legs.

She couldn't help checking out the other girls. She had a habit of comparing herself to others, especially when it came to riding. The best riders made riding look effortless, appearing to do nothing while sitting in the saddle. Those newer to the sport were easily identifiable by their flopping legs, pumping bodies, and bouncing hands.

A fresh wave of determination washed over her as her eyes locked on Alyssa, who appeared to be living up to her Top Rider status. She and Bentley looked like perfection as they trotted across the ground poles. McKenzie's posture was not quite as perfect and her smallish bay mare not quite as gorgeous, but they were solid nonetheless. Brynlei did not even recognize Anna. Anna stretched up tall in the saddle, keeping Rebel collected, although he clearly desired to go faster. With her blue hair hidden under her helmet, Anna blended into the prim and proper group of riders. She wondered if Anna liked that part of riding—of making her individuality disappear for a while so she and the horse could be judged solely on the quality of their performance.

Brynlei enjoyed that part of riding, too. Of course, she wouldn't want to stand out in a crowd in the first place. When she rode, she was in the zone. Riding forced her to focus on the moment, and only on the moment. To think too far ahead or worry about the past usually spelled disaster. She felt every step the horse took and every tug of his mouth against the reins. She concentrated on her position in the saddle, keeping her weight in her heels, her calves engaged, her shoulders tall, and her elbows bent. She focused on the lengthening or shortening of strides and on achieving a smooth transition from a walk to a canter or from a canter to a trot.

When jumping, Brynlei excelled at finding the perfect distance to each jump. She knew how to set a forward pace, keeping her horse straight down the lines and bending him through the corners. When they were three strides away from a jump, she had to make a decision: move her horse up to the jump, hold him steady, or collect him. Not making a decision was the worst thing she could do, as Terri had told her many times. Not making a decision was dangerous. With so many things to think about while riding, her mind could not wander from the task at hand. Riding quieted her mind and kept her present.

* * * *

After her first ride on Jett, Brynlei breathed a little easier. She knew her riding was up to par with the other girls, if not better. She was eager to figure out Jett's personality and quirks. The process of getting to know a new horse was like discovering a hidden part of herself. As she sprayed cool water on Jett behind the barn, two deer darted out of the woods and ran past them. Jett's eyes grew wild and white. He bolted sideways, snapping one of the quick release crossties off its ring. Brynlei grabbed the lead rope and clipped it to his halter. She reassured Jett in a calm voice and her demeanor soothed him, convincing him that there was nothing to fear. Jett's breathing slowed and he lowered his head. The deer weren't two monsters coming to eat him. Jett was fine. However, Brynlei couldn't see deer without remembering the night she watched one die.

A year before, Brynlei had witnessed something that opened a door to a darkness within her. A door that she could never fully close.

It was just after dinner. She rode in the passenger seat of her mom's candy apple-red-mini-van, as they cruised down the four-lane highway toward the grocery store. It was a last-minute outing. Her mom had run out of flour she needed for an order of cookies she was going to bake. Brynlei was out of shampoo, so she decided to go to the store with her mom. Out of nowhere, two deer bounded into the road up ahead, their light brown fur contrasting with the concrete road under their feet. As soon as she saw the deer, the dark energy enveloped Brynlei. She was going to see something she never wanted to see. The deer weren't supposed to be there. They were out of place amid the fenced-in subdivisions, sprawling strip malls, and glassy office buildings of suburban Detroit. Brynlei's mouth hung open, not able to scream, as the car in front of them slammed on its brakes and veered sharply to the right. It was too late. The car hit the first deer head-on, killing it instantly.

"No!" Brynlei yelled as their mini-van screeched to a halt. The worst was yet to come. The second deer's back legs had been crushed by the car. The deer was still alive and tried to pull itself across the road with its front legs, the back legs dragging behind.

"Oh, no." Her stomach lurched into her throat, as the deer's body flopped helplessly in the road. The deer's enormous eyes, like large brown saucers, looked directly at Brynlei, frantically searching for help. At that moment, Brynlei became the deer. She peered into the deer's soul in the moment before it left its body. She felt its helplessness, its fear, its knowledge that it was going to die.

Brynlei's mom turned on her flashers and pulled behind the car that had hit the deer.

"Don't look, honey," her mom said calmly, as if not looking would make it not happen.

More cars came to a halt behind them. After what seemed like an eternity, a police siren screeched through her head. The police car pulled up next to them, its spinning lights blinding her eyes. An officer stepped out and walked over to the struggling deer. He held his gun steadily in both hands and shot the deer in the head with a sickening BANG. Hot tears burned like lava down Brynlei's face. He may as well have shot her.

They eventually made it to the grocery store, but Brynlei waited in the car. She replayed the nauseating scene over and over in her head. She couldn't get the deer's pleading eyes out of her mind. Or the energy of the deer's frantic terror. It ripped through her heart. If only she could have done something to help it.

Two weeks later, she still thought about the deer constantly. How many other animals were meeting the same fate on highways every day? The agony of each imagined death shot through her body. Brynlei kept to herself even more than usual. That Friday night, she turned down a sleepover at Rebecca's house.

"Is something bothering you, Brynlei," her mom asked after another silent drive home from the barn.

"I can't stop thinking about that deer."

Her mom's head whipped toward her, eyes wide with shock. "That was two weeks ago. You can't control what wild animals do. You just have to move on." She paused to regain her composure. "The important thing is that no one was hurt."

"What do you mean no one was hurt?" Brynlei's blood surged through her veins. "The deer was hurt! He was so scared. Did you see his face? He didn't know what was happening!" Tears filled her eyes once again.

Brynlei's mom studied her daughter's face, as if trying to figure out if Brynlei's irrational thoughts came from her side of the family, or if her husband's genetics were to blame. Apparently, it didn't matter. She put her arms around Brynlei and gave her a much-needed hug.

A few hours later, Brynlei decided to become a vegetarian. She could never be responsible for an animal suffering the kind of torment that she saw on the road that night. Yes, animals would still be treated cruelly and suffer and die at the hands of humans, but at least she would not be responsible. After she made the decision to become a vegetarian, she slept more soundly than she had in two weeks.

The next morning, she sat at the breakfast table, sipping orange juice. Her mom, dad, and brother bustled around her with their morning routines.

"I'm going to be a vegetarian," she announced, out of nowhere. Like a helium balloon about to pop, she couldn't keep the good news to herself.

Derek laughed loudly. "Great. More bacon for me!"

Brynlei's mom and dad stopped and stared at her.

"Is this about the deer, honey?" The deep creases in her mom's forehead made her appear years older.

That night after dinner, her parents sat her down on the living room couch.

"We need to talk," her mom started. Brynlei knew she would not like whatever was coming next. Brynlei called Maverick over to her and scratched behind his soft ears, pretending to ignore the fact that her parents sat across from her, staring.

"We're worried about you, Bryn," her dad said. "You shouldn't be this upset about a couple of deer getting hit by a car. It happens every day."

"Is that supposed to make me feel better?" Brynlei's heart pumped faster. "People get murdered every day, too. Does that make it okay?"

Her parents looked straight ahead, not responding. After a loud sigh and an awkward pause, they told her about a psychologist who came highly recommended from one of her dad's clients. They had already set up an appointment for Brynlei to meet with the woman tomorrow after school.

Brynlei's face burned. She felt like a thermometer that was just thrown into a pot of boiling water. She did not know if she was angrier about her parents' thinking there was something wrong with her or them talking to other people about her behind her back. She instinctively flung her arms around Maverick and pulled him close to her. He was the only one who hadn't betrayed her.

"She can help you with whatever is bothering you," her mom tried to reassure her.

"There's nothing wrong with me." Brynlei buried her face in Maverick's furry neck.

"You're right. There isn't," her dad said. "At least you can talk to her about whatever is making you sad. It will make you feel better."

"I can talk to Rebecca," Brynlei said.

"Yes, but you haven't been talking to Rebecca lately either." Her mom sat with her hands folded. Her mom had a response for everything, as if she'd rehearsed the whole conversation earlier.

Brynlei couldn't argue with them. She had been keeping to herself lately. When she'd tried telling Rebecca about the deer, Rebecca had cracked a joke about Bambi kabobs. For two weeks, Brynlei had been tormented by constant thoughts of the suffering deer. She knew no one else would understand. Not even Rebecca or a psychologist.

As it turned out, Brynlei was wrong on both counts.

Chapter Six

The following afternoon, Brynlei sank into the surprisingly comfortable velvety couch in Mindy Preston's office. Framed awards and diplomas hung impressively on the wall in a neat row. The psychologist appeared to be about the same age as Brynlei's parents.

"Please call me Mindy," she said, as she sat in a chair opposite Brynlei with a clipboard and pen in her hands. Mindy's light hair was pulled back in a low bun, and thick black-framed glassed rested on her nose. Despite her professional demeanor, she had a friendly smile. Brynlei could see how people felt comfortable opening up to someone like her. Mindy carried a few extra pounds and wore a wool sweater that looked more like a blanket with a hole in the middle. Brynlei never understood that kind of sweater. "Is it a blanket, or is it a sweater?" she would have joked with Rebecca under different circumstances.

Mindy scribbled something on her clipboard. "So, Brynlei, tell me why you think your parents wanted you to come talk to me?"

"I'm not really sure," Brynlei said, wondering if this was a trick question. "I mean, I guess they think something is bothering me."

"Is something bothering you?" Mindy leaned in closer.

"Yes. A lot of things bother me."

"Can you give me some examples?" Mindy prodded.

Brynlei pressed her hands down into the squishy couch. "Like, a couple weeks ago, when I saw two deer get run over. That bothered me." Mindy nodded as if she knew exactly what Brynlei was talking about.

"Especially the one that didn't die right away. I saw that it was scared and hurt," Brynlei continued. "I wanted to help it, but I couldn't."

"How did that make you feel?" Brynlei had a feeling Mindy already

46

knew all the answers to the questions she was asking.

"I felt scared and hurt, just like the deer. I love animals," Brynlei added, explaining the obvious.

"That must have been a painful experience for you." Mindy's unflinching blue-gray eyes revealed genuine concern. "Do you think about that accident a lot?"

"Yes."

"What other things do you think about a lot?"

"Horses," Brynlei said without thinking. "I ride."

"So that's a positive thing that you think about?"

"Yes."

"That's a great hobby to have," Mindy said. "Horses are known to have many healing qualities."

Brynlei couldn't think of anything to say. There was a long silence. She lightened the pressure on her hands and wondered if she'd left permanent handprints on the cushion next to her legs.

"Are there any other negative things that you think about often?" Mindy said.

"Yes." Brynlei didn't know where to start. "Like, if someone at school says something mean to me, I can't just shake it off. It really hurts me."

Mindy nodded.

"Or, even if I hear someone say something mean to someone else, that hurts me too. Or if I see something on TV, like a storm that wipes out a town or kids starving in Africa, I feel really sad." Brynlei's voice cracked as she envisioned the horrible events.

"Do you feel like these events affect you more than they affect other people?" Mindy asked.

"Yes. I know they affect me more. No one else seems to care. My mom thinks that if you just ignore the bad stuff then it's like it didn't really happen."

"Do you think that's a way she might protect herself from all of the bad things in the world?" Mindy suggested.

"I guess," Brynlei conceded.

"Have you ever thought about hurting yourself? Or taking your life?"

"No." *Woah. Where was this coming from?* Brynlei crossed her arms and tried to sit up straighter in the couch.

"Do you have many friends at school?" Mindy asked.

"Yes. I mean, I'm not Miss Popularity, but I have a few friends. Rebecca is my best friend."

"How do you feel around large groups of people?"

"I don't like it. I feel like I don't fit. I can feel their eyes on me, like everyone is judging me," Brynlei said.

Their conversation continued for several more minutes. Mindy began asking Brynlei questions about her sensitivity to light, noise, and smells, whether she contributed to class discussions or preferred one-on-one conversations.

She told Mindy about her first time going to gym class in kindergarten. How the bouncing balls on the floor boomed like thunder. How the other kids ran around, happily yelling and chasing each other, while the loud echoes of the yells and bouncing balls attacked Brynlei's senses. How she felt like she was exposed on a battlefield, being bombed from above. How she ran to the corner of the gym and cowered, crying. How the other kids and even the gym teacher couldn't understand why she was crying. How she couldn't understand why everyone else wasn't crying, too.

"Brynlei, do you ever notice things, maybe even tiny details others seem to miss?" Mindy said.

Brynlei wanted to jump off the pillow-laden sofa and scream, Yes. All the time. Instead, she sat motionless, as the couch slowly swallowed her like quicksand.

She politely told Mindy about Derek's car accident from a few months earlier. Then she remembered her eighth birthday, which had fallen two weeks after her grandma died. She recounted for Mindy how she had sat with her parents and brother in the living room, opening presents. How everyone was pretending to be happy, even though Brynlei knew they were sad.

How she left the room to go to the bathroom and when she came back a minute later, her grandma was sitting in the light-blue chair in the corner of the living room wearing her favorite red dress with the little bows on the sleeves. How her grandma looked at her and smiled, how she appeared to be a real person, just as real as Mindy was sitting there now. Brynlei had looked around the room to see the excitement on everyone's faces, only to realize that no one else could see her grandma. Only Brynlei could see her. Then just as fast as her grandma appeared, she was gone. Brynlei admitted that she still sat in the light-blue chair whenever she wanted to feel close to her grandma, how she could still feel her grandma's energy surround her.

Mindy nodded her head up and down as she followed along with Brynlei's story.

"Brynlei, with your permission I'd like to ask your mom to join us for the last ten minutes of your session," Mindy said.

A minute later, Brynlei's mom sank into the couch next to her, a forced smile plastered to her face. Mindy proceeded to tell them that, in her professional opinion, Brynlei did not need ongoing therapy or medication. Mindy believed Brynlei was a Highly Sensitive Person or HSP. Mindy explained that HSPs account for about fifteen to twenty percent of the population.

"HSPs process sensory data much more deeply due to a biological difference in their nervous systems." Mindy smiled at Brynlei. "It's nothing to be alarmed by. In the past, HSPs were sometimes confused with having innate shyness or social anxiety problems. Now we know that some people like you, Brynlei, are just more easily stimulated by the world. Some HSPs may even have what some describe as a sixth sense. It sounds to me like you fall into this category. I'd say you're at the extreme end of the HSP spectrum."

As Brynlei listened to Mindy describe the common traits of HSPs, it was as if Mindy was describing her. Someone finally understood her feelings. Her body lightened as a flood of relief poured through her. She wasn't crazy. She couldn't wait to tell Rebecca.

"While there is nothing clinically wrong with Brynlei, there are things you can do to make dealing with her sensitivities easier for her," Mindy continued, now addressing Brynlei's mom. "Limit exposure to television, especially the news. There's no reason she needs to absorb all of the horrible things going on in the world every day. Brynlei should stick to a routine. She'll likely need some down time every day in order recharge."

Mindy gave a few more pieces of advice. She handed Brynlei's mom a list of recommended reading, entitled How to Deal with your Highly Sensitive Child. The squishy couch rose and fell as her mom breathed a sigh of relief. Brynlei was relieved, too.

That night, she and Rebecca sat on Brynlei's bed. Brynlei recounted every detail of her conversation with the psychologist. This time, when she mentioned the deer in the road, Rebecca didn't crack any jokes. She told Rebecca about her decision to become a vegetarian and about being diagnosed as a Highly Sensitive Person. Rebecca listened intently with wide eyes, nodding her head every once in a while. After what seemed like an hour, Brynlei stopped talking.

"This is amazing," Rebecca said, smiling widely. "You're a super-feeler."

They both had laughed, not yet aware where Brynlei's sensitivities would lead her.

* * * *

After lunch, Brynlei lay in her bunk in Cabin 5. There was an hour and a half of free time before the group trail ride. A box fan wedged in the window blew warm air in her direction. Her muscles twitched from the two-hour riding lesson earlier that morning. Layers of dirt and dried sweat clung to her warm, sticky skin. It would be heaven to take a shower, but she didn't see the point in getting clean until after the trail ride.

Alyssa and McKenzie sat on their beds and gossiped about a girl who rode at their barn back in Chicago. Apparently, the girl was a hundred pounds overweight and had somehow managed to get pregnant. Alyssa and McKenzie couldn't fathom it.

"Who would have sex with her?" Alyssa screeched.

"That's so gross." McKenzie crinkled her nose.

"And her poor horse," Alyssa said. "He looks like he's in pain every time she rides him."

"I hope her parents make her sell him," McKenzie agreed.

The other girls in Cabin 5, even Brynlei, snickered along with Alyssa and McKenzie. They hadn't met the unfortunate girl, but she was an easy target. Brynlei's heart secretly ached for the girl, having to deal with Alyssa and McKenzie laughing at her every time she went to the barn to ride her horse.

Alyssa announced she and McKenzie were heading to the beach. Brynlei closed her eyes, trying to suppress her smile. Kaitlyn went with them, but Julia, Anna, and Brynlei stayed behind, too tired to leave their bunks. All three girls lay on their beds plugged into their ear buds and listening to music on their iPods. Brynlei read the latest issue of *Practical Horseman* magazine on her eReader. She loved the section where George Morris judged the form of four different riders at the same point over a jump. She tried to rank the riders in the correct order before reading verdict.

A thump echoed in the hallway. Brynlei took out one of her ear buds and craned her neck toward the door. Hopefully, the other three girls hadn't returned already. They'd only been gone for twenty minutes and she needed her quiet time. The low drone of the fan was the only noise in the cabin. It was probably the wind. She replaced her ear bud and went back to reading.

When the girls returned from the beach thirty minutes later, Brynlei awoke with a start. She must have been more tired than she realized. Brynlei needed to freshen up and put on a new shirt before the trail ride. She walked down the hallway to Cabin 5's communal bathroom and pulled her kit from the shelf. She sifted through the items inside, searching for the deodorant she'd packed. Tom's of Maine, her favorite brand. It wasn't there. Hadn't she put it back in her kit after getting dressed in the morning? Yes, she remembered putting it away. She searched the shelves in the bathroom, but her deodorant wasn't there either. She pulled a clean shirt over her head and went back into the bunkroom.

"Has anyone seen my deodorant?" Brynlei said. "Tom's of Maine?" It was a weird question.

"Nope," Julia said.

"I can't find it. I thought it was in my kit."

"Someone probably took it," Alyssa said. "Some loser stole my shampoo and conditioner last year. This year I'm keeping my bathroom kit under my bunk."

"Either that, or the ghost of Caroline took it," Julia added.

"Why would a ghost need deodorant?" Anna asked.

"Yeah, I mean, seriously. How could a ghost even sweat?" Kaitlyn added with a laugh. "I have an extra one, Brynlei. Seriously, you can have it." Kaitlyn dug out a spare stick of deodorant from her purple duffel bag and handed it to Brynlei.

"Thanks." Brynlei took the white and pink plastic tube from Kaitlyn. It wasn't Tom's of Maine, but she was grateful nonetheless.

"Yeah, thanks from all of us," Anna said, fanning her hand in front of her nose.

All the girls laughed. From behind her forced smile, Brynlei scanned the room and wondered who had gone through her things.

* * * *

Miss Jill and her spirited gray mare, Breezy, led the Flying Foxes and Happy Hunters on their first trail ride through the woods surrounding Foxwoode. Brynlei relaxed in the saddle as Jett ambled along the narrow, dusty path. Patches of afternoon sunlight filtered through the tree branches and formed moving patterns on Jett's black coat. The flowing patterns of light resembled a silent movie Brynlei had watched once in sixth grade. Times must have been so different back when the movie was made. Different and simpler. She and Jett were toward the back of the line of horses, behind Anna and Rebel. Kaitlyn and Julia were on their horses behind Brynlei. Miss Ashley and her chestnut Warmblood, Anakin, brought up the rear.

There was enough space between the horses so that Brynlei could pretend that she and Jett were trekking alone. The peaceful ride through the wilderness was a treat. At the barn where she rode at home, she was resigned to riding in an outdoor ring or an indoor arena in the winter months. The trails that used to exist around the barn had been replaced by concrete and vinyl. Over the years, she'd watched with despair as developers gradually bought up the farmland and forested areas surrounding the barn. Each wooded lot they leveled was like losing a piece of herself. Each field they dug up and poured with concrete was like a cancer slowly spreading. They popped up soulless subdivisions, one after another. She hated how they named the subdivisions things like Steeplechase and Trail Head, as if they wanted to memorialize what they had destroyed. Brynlei worried her barn would sell out to the developers. She already drove forty minutes to get to the barn, and it was the closest one to her house. Soon she'd be driving an hour or more to find farmland developers hadn't yet converted to endless, generic housing. Terri assured her that all of the stalls were full and the barn was making money. The white fences surrounding the pastures seemed to hold the developers at bay for now.

Brynlei took in the majestic scenery and wished she could live someplace like this. Someplace with so much open land and dense forest that real estate developers wouldn't dare to conquer it. Someplace safe from the traffic and strip malls and crowds. She dreamed of living in a luxurious log cabin house on a big piece of land with her own horse barn in the back.

"Exactly how will you afford that?" her mom would ask her in a sarcastic voice whenever Brynlei had approached the topic.

Brynlei didn't have the answer to that one yet, but she vowed to figure something out. She still had a few years to work on it. Then there was Rebecca's stock response.

"You'll just have to marry a millionaire." Brynlei was never sure if Rebecca was joking or serious when she said that.

Her mind had drifted to what her future millionaire husband would look like.

Jett plodded rhythmically through the pristine landscape. The earthy scent of pine needles, tree moss, and raspberries filled Brynlei's senses. Wild raspberry bushes sprouted up along the trail, their thorns threatening to impale anyone who reached for the ripe fruit. A small creek with crystal clear water babbled to the right of the trail. She could see straight through the rushing water to the leaves and stones on the bottom.

Anna turned back toward Brynlei. "We're stopping for minute to let the horses drink from the creek. Pass it on."

Brynlei passed the same message back to Kaitlyn. She guided Jett over to the creek and let him stretch his head toward the water. Out of the corner of her eye, Brynlei saw something dart behind one of the trees in the distance. She would have dismissed it as a squirrel or a deer, but it was too tall. It almost looked like a person, but then it was gone. The hairs on Brynlei's neck stood on end. The dark energy prickled her skin. She could feel someone watching her. Jett jerked his head up and perked his ears toward the trees beyond the creek. His nostrils flared and his feet danced. He was on alert and so was Brynlei.

"Did you see that?" Brynlei said to Anna. Rebel stopped drinking and danced nervously, too.

"No, but something is spooking the horses."

"I swear I just saw someone run behind those trees back there," Brynlei said.

Anna looked again, searching the trees.

"I don't see anything. Why would someone be all the way out here?"

"I don't know." Brynlei sat motionless atop Jett, trying to discern any movement in the woods.

"Maybe it was a deer," Anna offered.

"Yeah, maybe." Brynlei knew it wasn't a deer. The shadow she saw was too tall. As they continued on the trail ride, Brynlei felt eyes burning a hole into her back.

* * * *

Brynlei lay in her bunk, unable to sleep. The swirling fan buzzed in her ears. She found it difficult to push back all of the questions that continued to pop into her head. The thoughts that circled her mind were like the Whack-A-Mole game she used to play as a child. As soon as she pounded down one worry, another one popped up. She'd only been at Foxwoode for three days, yet so much had already happened. How would she make it through three weeks?

She tried to remember everything about the story Alyssa told them at the bonfire. Was it possible the ghost of Caroline Watson really haunted the woods? She'd glimpsed a human figure three times already. All three times the figure had disappeared before she could get a good look. Had she seen Caroline's ghost? Maybe Caroline really did want someone to find her body so she could rest in peace.

Alyssa said Caroline had long black hair and green eyes, but Brynlei hadn't seen any of the details of the figure behind the tree. Maybe someone else was out there. Why hadn't anyone else noticed? Brynlei remembered the psychologist's words from a year ago—highly sensitive people often have a sixth sense and notice things that others miss. Perhaps other people had seen Caroline, but Brynlei was the only one who was perceptive enough to notice.

Now, her deodorant was missing. That really didn't make sense. Anyone could buy a stick of deodorant in Foxwoode's store. Maybe she had just misplaced it and it would turn up in a couple days when she least expected it. She wished she could talk to Rebecca, or at least text her. Rebecca would be in heaven making fun of The Case of the Missing Deodorant. Without any cell phone reception, she couldn't contact Rebecca unless she used the phone in the office. Anyway, Rebecca was heading off to music camp for the next two weeks and would be too busy to discuss possible ghost stories or misplaced sticks of deodorant.

As thoughts continued to shuffle through her head, a shadowy Miss Jill opened the door and stepped into the cabin. Midnight bunk check. Brynlei lay still and closed her eyes, pretending to be asleep. This sleeping act was becoming her nightly routine. Miss Jill paused and then stepped out, closing the door gently behind her. The whirring fan only barely drowned out the labored breathing of the sleeping girls around Brynlei. The more she tried not to hear their breathing, the more she noticed it.

Brynlei flipped over on her stomach in frustration. She was so tired. Possibly more tired than she'd ever been in her entire life. Why couldn't she fall asleep? The evenly-spaced wooden slats above the bunk slowly rose up and down with Anna's breathing. At last, Brynlei's eyelids drooped with heaviness. As she edged closer to sleep, a floorboard creaked in the hallway. Her eyes popped open and an ice-cold chill ran through her body. She craned her neck to look toward the sound. The bathroom light was on. It didn't make sense. No one had gotten out of bed. No one had opened the door. She would have heard the door open and close if Miss Jill had returned. How was it possible?

She waited silently, afraid to breathe or even blink. No sound reached her, except for the spinning fan and the breathing girls. Finally, she took a deep breath and swung her legs over the side of her bed. She needed to investigate or she'd never fall asleep. Just as her bare feet touched the wooden floor, the bathroom light flipped off, returning the cabin to complete blackness. Brynlei froze for a second, another dark warning prickling over her skin. Her eyes were still adjusting to the darkness as she bolted to the bathroom and pushed open the door. She flipped on the light. No one was there.

Brynlei's mouth hung open in disbelief. How had the light turned on and off by itself? She knew from watching plenty of ghost hunter shows on TV that sometimes these things had a logical explanation. Maybe it was a faulty light bulb or a short-circuit. Yes, those things made sense. For tonight, Brynlei had to be satisfied with that answer. She made a mental note to mention it to Anna tomorrow. She climbed back into her bed, pulled the covers over her head, and closed her eyes. Eventually, the heavy blanket of sleep enveloped her.

Chapter Seven

Brynlei ate a quick breakfast and arrived at the barn a few minutes earlier than the other girls. The dust floating in the barn glistened in the morning sun like tiny snowflakes. She breathed in the scent of freshly-cut hay layered with cedar and the earthy smell of horses.

Although her body felt heavy from her restless night, she was determined not let her lack of sleep affect her riding. She carefully lifted Jett's hooves, one by one, and cleaned them out with her hoof pick. Then she ran the currycomb over his body in small, circular motions. Nothing relaxed her like brushing a horse. As Brynlei bent down to pull a soft brush out of her caddy, the barn hand, Bruce, pushed a wheelbarrow full of hay past her. The horses whinnied at the sound of the wheelbarrow creaking down the aisle. They knew what was coming.

She looked up and smiled awkwardly at Bruce. Barn hands always made her uncomfortable, especially the male ones. She didn't want to be overly friendly, but she didn't want them to think she looked down on them either. After seeing the way Bruce dealt with Alyssa on the first day, Brynlei sensed he was a good person. He'd probably been dealt a difficult hand in life.

Bruce nodded at her without changing his expression and pushed the wheelbarrow to the end of the aisle. Brynlei imagined her dad saying, "I wouldn't want to play poker with that guy." That was one of his favorite lines whenever he couldn't read someone. She wouldn't be surprised if people said that about her, too. She kept her emotions guarded. The way she felt inside was nobody's business but her own.

A scraggly-looking black and tan dog trotted after Bruce. Maybe part Rottweiler, part shepherd, but it was hard to tell. Her heart ached for

Maverick.

"Sit, Ranger," Bruce said to the dog. Ranger sat and waited obediently as Bruce slid open the stall doors one at a time, tossing a flake of hay into each stall. She liked the way Bruce said good morning to each horse as he threw in the hay. He was obviously more comfortable talking to animals than to people. Brynlei could relate to that.

She brushed Jett until the muscles in her arm burned. His black coat would gleam today. She was going to wrap his legs in white polo wraps to contrast with his perfect blackness.

Bruce slowly made his way back down the aisle toward her. When he finished throwing the hay into the last stall he said, "Ranger, come."

Ranger bounded toward Bruce with his tongue flapping and his tail wagging as a black barn cat darted across the aisle. Brynlei couldn't help chuckling at the joyful dog. His panting tongue made him look as if he was laughing.

"What kind of dog is he?" Brynlei said when she heard Bruce laughing too.

"No idea," Bruce responded. "Found 'em wanderin' around here three summers ago. None of the girls would take 'em home, so I kept 'em. Been following me ever since."

"He's cute."

Bruce shuffled his feet and stared at the ground, looking uncomfortable, like he had said too much. Maybe he didn't know what to say next. The blank expression returned to his face. He nodded again at Brynlei and pushed the wheelbarrow to the next aisle. Ranger followed closely behind.

* * * *

A few minutes later, girls began to filter through the barn door. The barn aisles filled with high-pitched chatter, as everyone began the process of grooming and tacking-up their horses. Anna led Rebel into the grooming stall next to Jett.

"Jett's looking handsome today," Anna said. "The white polo wraps are a nice touch."

"Thanks. I brought them from home." Brynlei took a step back to admire her work.

"I heard we're doing gymnastics today," Anna said. "Should be interesting on Rebel."

Gymnastics exercises in riding referred to a series of jumps, each placed less than three strides apart from the next. The quick succession of jumps forced the horse and rider to focus on balance and position.

"You've handled him well so far," Brynlei said. "I'm sure you'll do great."

Anna smiled. "Yeah, you haven't looked too horrible either."

Brynlei had been pleased with her rides in the last three lessons and hoped she could ride as well today.

"I saw on the schedule that we have free ride time tomorrow afternoon," Brynlei said. "Do you want to go on a trail ride together?"

Foxwoode demanded the buddy system for all trail rides. The girls and instructors were also required to log their trail ride route on the clipboard in the barn before they left so people would know where they were in case of an emergency. After what happened to Caroline Watson, no one dared to argue with those rules.

"Yeah, sure. As long as you don't creep me out by seeing strange people hiding behind the trees again."

Brynlei laughed. She wouldn't tell Anna this, but deep down, she did want to see the person in the woods again. She couldn't stop wondering who it was and why he or she was out there. Could the ghost story about Caroline Watson be true? Brynlei shivered at the thought of the bathroom light turning on and off by itself in the middle of the night. Now probably wasn't a good time to tell Anna about that. She didn't want to scare her away.

* * * *

Out in Ring A, Miss Jill arranged four jumps into a line while the Flying Foxes warmed up. As Brynlei trotted Jett around the perimeter of the ring, she envisioned yesterday's lesson in her head. Miss Jill had set up a simple line of jumps. She told the girls to begin with a collected five strides down the line and then circle back around to the same line to get four strides the next time and then five strides and then back to four strides. Some of the girls struggled at first with the exercise, but Brynlei made her strides the first time, instantly earning some respect from the others in her group. Because of yesterday's success adjusting Jett's stride, her stomach didn't feel as jittery this morning. She couldn't wait to get started with the gymnastics exercise.

As usual, Miss Jill critiqued the girls' riding at the walk, trot, and canter for the first thirty minutes. After the flat work, they were allowed a short water break. Sweat dripped down Brynlei's face as she grabbed the bottle she'd balanced on the fence post and gulped down half of it. While Brynlei swallowed the lukewarm water, she noticed Bruce kneeling on the ground outside the ring. He worked methodically, replacing rotten pieces of wood with fresh boards. Her eyes caught Bruce's, and they stared at each other for a second before both quickly looked away.

Miss Jill gave Brynlei the order to jump first. Brynlei listened carefully to the instructions. She was to trot in over a small X, canter two strides to the next vertical, bounce over the third jump, and then take one stride before the last jump. It looked fairly straightforward, although she wasn't sure how Jett would handle the bounce, which meant there were no strides between the two jumps—just a landing and taking off again. Brynlei picked up a forward trot and circled Jett toward the first jump, keeping her eyes up, always looking beyond the jump. Jett approached slightly crooked, but Brynlei straightened him out and moved him forward enough to make the two strides easily. She sat up, held her position for the bounce and then closed her legs for the final stride.

"Excellent, Brynlei." Miss Jill beamed. "Great job holding your position through the fences and keeping contact with his mouth. Make sure to keep him moving straight and forward to the first trot jump. Create a tunnel with your legs and push him through."

Brynlei nodded her head, relieved that her first round had gone smoothly. Alyssa and Bentley were up next. They completed the line easily, but Bentley rushed the last jump and barely fit in a stride.

"Great, until the last jump," Miss Jill yelled to Alyssa. "Hold him steady next time." Alyssa nodded.

One by one, each of the girls tackled the exercise. McKenzie's mare stopped in the middle of the line.

Julia and Devon made it down the line, but it wasn't pretty.

Kaitlyn and Daisey didn't have enough speed going in and added an extra stride between the first and second jumps.

Anna was the last to go. She trotted Rebel forward toward the X, her eyes up and shoulders back. The first jump was perfect. Anna steadied Rebel to the second jump, and then the bounce. Rebel's ears twitched and his tail swished wildly. Just before the final jump, Rebel bolted sideways, leaving Anna clinging to his neck. Anna quickly regained her composure and lowered herself back into the saddle.

"He has a habit of ducking out on jumps, Anna." Miss Jill sounded annoyed, as if Anna should have known. "Do it again, please. Keep him tunneled straight. Don't give him an option of running out."

The next time Anna went down the line, she rode it perfectly. Brynlei admired Anna's ability to learn from her mistakes. The lesson continued for another forty-five minutes, with each horse and rider team completing the gymnastics exercise several times. Miss Jill raised the jumps halfway through the exercise to make it more difficult. Bruce continued to replace boards along the neighboring fence line. He glanced toward Ring A every so often, as if keeping track of their progress during the lesson. Brynlei wondered if Bruce ever got to ride the horses he cared for or if he was resigned to watch others ride while he worked.

"Everyone walk out your horses and then hose them down with cool water." Miss Jill spoke through a sly smile, like she'd just proven to the girls that they still had a lot to learn. "For free ride tomorrow, I encourage you to swap horses with a friend. You can ride in the ring or on the trail; it doesn't matter. By teaching someone else to ride your horse, you're also reinforcing your own knowledge."

Anna glanced at Brynlei. "Looks like you're riding Rebel on our trail ride tomorrow."

* * * *

The Flying Foxes sat at a wooden table with a red-and-white-checkered tablecloth in the corner of the mess hall's dining room. Alyssa sat across from Brynlei and picked at the grilled chicken salad she had just assembled at the salad bar. It had taken some time, but Brynlei was feeling more comfortable around her cabin mates. She enjoyed talking to Anna, who was down to earth and had interesting perspectives on things. Anna didn't feel the need to spit out every thought that popped into her head. Brynlei appreciated that. Julia and Kaitlyn were nice. They were funny and always made an effort to include Brynlei in their conversations, although Kaitlyn's overuse of the word seriously and Julia's mumbling were slightly annoying. McKenzie was okay, too, when she wasn't trying to be something she wasn't. When McKenzie was with Alyssa, Brynlei wanted to grab her by the shoulders, shake her, and ask her why she followed Alyssa around like a puppy dog. Did she really strive to be as fake and shallow as Alyssa? It was pathetic.

Alyssa with her shrill voice, constant judgment of others, and condescending attitude was something else. Every word out of her mouth assaulted Brynlei's senses like knives stabbing her everywhere. It was possible her negative feeling toward Alyssa came from jealousy. After all, Alyssa was attractive, owned a herd of fancy horses, was a great rider, and had parents who were willing to spend endless amounts of money to support her habit. No. That wasn't it. Brynlei really didn't like her.

"Is it just me, or was Bruce totally creeping you guys out during our lesson this morning?" Alyssa asked, flipping her blond hair back over her shoulder.

"Yeah, he was staring at us," McKenzie said. "Ew."

"I didn't notice it," Brynlei responded, even though she had. She suddenly wanted to defend Bruce from their viciousness. "I mean, I saw him working on the fence. He had to look somewhere."

"He's just doing his job, guys," Anna said. "Leave the poor guy alone."

"Do you think he really could have killed that Caroline girl?" Julia almost whispered, leaning in close.

"It wouldn't surprise me," Alyssa said. "There's definitely something off with that guy, and I'm not just talking about the clothes he wears." Alyssa laughed loudly.

McKenzie laughed, too. Those two always seemed to laugh the loudest when it was at someone else's expense.

"I'm sure they wouldn't let him work here if he was a suspect in Caroline's death," Anna said, before stuffing a forkful of spinach salad into her mouth.

"That's not true." Alyssa shook her head. "He's somehow related to the Olsons. I think he's their nephew. They would believe whatever he told them. Anyway, the police are so stupid. They say that Bruce had an alibi for the day Caroline disappeared. That he was volunteering at the Humane Society when she went missing, but he could have had someone lie for him. It's so easy to trick the police."

"How do you know how easy it is to trick the police, Alyssa?" Anna said, raising an eyebrow.

"I see people do it all the time on TV. I watch Dateline and CSI. I just know." Alyssa continued picking at her salad. Brynlei wondered if Alyssa knew how stupid she sounded.

"Do you know he still volunteers at the Humane Society once a week?" Kaitlyn said. "Seriously, he told me yesterday when I was asking him about Ranger."

"He seems to really love animals," Brynlei added, trying to turn the conversation in Bruce's favor.

"Yeah, he loves them so much that he drops them all at Foxwoode right before they're about to be killed at the shelter." Alyssa glanced over her shoulder and then leaned closer. "My instructor last summer, Miss Elizabeth, told me that she saw Bruce outside the barn at four in the morning, releasing two stray cats from a pet carrier. After that, she realized where all the stray cats and dogs at Foxwoode were coming from. They weren't just wandering over to Foxwoode by accident. He drops them here and then hopes that one of us will fall in love with them and take them home. That's how he ended up with Ranger. No one took him, so Bruce had to adopt him himself."

Brynlei's jaw dropped open before she covered her mouth with her hand. That was actually a really good idea. Bruce had probably found homes for dozens of animals who would have otherwise been killed.

"Miss Elizabeth also told me that she reported what she saw to the Olsons. They told her they already had a suspicion Bruce was releasing the stray animals, but that they preferred to let it slide. They viewed it as harmless and asked her to keep the information to herself." Alyssa narrowed her eyes. "Miss Elizabeth isn't back this summer." She paused for effect. "I'm just saying."

"I wonder what else Bruce does that they let slide," McKenzie said.

"That's exactly what I mean." Alyssa nodded slowly. "He could have gotten away with murder."

"Nothing against Bruce," Anna said, "but he doesn't seem like the smartest guy in the room. I really don't think he could have pulled something like that off without leaving any evidence behind."

"Maybe, maybe not." Alyssa shrugged. "There are hundreds and hundreds of acres of woods surrounding us. The evidence could be anywhere. Maybe the police didn't know where to look."

"Because they're stupid," Anna finished, rolling her eyes.

"Right." Alyssa gulped down the last of her Diet Coke.

Chapter Eight

On Wednesday afternoon, Brynlei recorded her name, Anna's name, the time, and the trail that they would follow in the log on the barn wall. All of the trails at Foxwoode were marked by occasional yellow, green, blue, or orange neon signs nailed to the trees. Brynlei couldn't help thinking of a similarly marked trail system that she and Rebecca had hiked together at the nature center last spring.

"This is just how the Native Americans used to find their way," Rebecca had joked. She smiled at the thought of Rebecca.

Brynlei and Anna would take the Blue trail, which was the same route they had followed with the group on Monday. At a walk, it would take about two and a half hours to complete the loop. As Miss Jill had suggested the day before, Brynlei and Anna were riding each other's horses. Clouds thickened in the sky as Anna guided Jett past a neon blue sign and into an opening in the trees ahead. Brynlei and Rebel followed a horse-length behind. The daylight darkened five shades as they entered the forest, as if someone was sliding down a dimmer switch on the sun.

Rebel danced and pranced every time a twig cracked in the woods. Brynlei made an effort to remain composed to calm Rebel. She sat back in the saddle and breathed deeply, trying to relax and enjoy the scenic surroundings.

It didn't seem possible for trees to be so tall and the forest so dense. A chipmunk scurried up a tree a few feet off the trail. Rebel sprung to the side and galloped for a step before Brynlei pulled him back to a walk. The horse tossed his head and his nostrils flared. Brynlei laughed.

"What's wrong with your horse?" she said to Anna. "He's scared of a chipmunk."

"He's crazy. I think that's why they matched me with him."

She and Anna talked about the different personality traits of their horses as they rode and tried to predict how their horses would react in different situations. They both agreed that Rebel would refuse to jump a water jump because he would be scared of his own reflection, while Jett would leap extra-high over it for fear of getting his perfectly polished hooves wet.

They poked fun at themselves for wearing synthetic leather boots, while Alyssa and the other girls wore tall boots that probably cost as much as their horses. They both agreed that synthetic leather was better than the real thing, for so many different reasons.

"Alyssa and McKenzie think I'm here on scholarship." A sheepish grin spread across Anna's face.

"Yeah. I know." Brynlei smiled, too, remembering her dad's sarcastic comment about making too much money.

"They can think that if they want. It would be awesome to be here on scholarship. That would mean that I really earned it."

"Yeah." Brynlei looked down at the dusty trail passing beneath her as she rode.

"Alyssa is an idiot." Anna wasn't ready to leave it alone yet.

"Her soul isn't evolved. This is probably her first life." The words escaped Brynlei's mouth before she had a chance to filter them.

Anna pulled Jett to a halt. "What did you say?"

Brynlei's face grew warm. "I said Alyssa doesn't have an evolved soul. That means she hasn't lived any past lives. I believe in past lives."

"I LOVE that shit." Anna's eyes bulged wide with excitement.

Brynlei breathed a sigh of relief. She and Anna had more in common than she thought. They continued plodding along the trail, Brynlei telling Anna everything she's learned about past lives, how past lives explain the feeling of déjà vu people get all the time, how past lives account for passions and seemingly irrational fears. Anna listened in silence, nodding her head in agreement.

"I saw this documentary about a guy who loved bears so much that he went to live with them in Alaska," Anna finally interjected. "He did everything with them—ate, bathed, slept—and he filmed it all. But after about a year, something happened and one of the bears ate him."

"Oh, my God!"

"Who do you think that guy would come back as? Would he still love bears in his next life? Or would he be deathly afraid of them?"

"He probably came back as a bear." The answer seemed obvious to Brynlei.

While they rode on along the trail, Brynlei scanned the trees for signs of movement. She searched while they talked, not wanting to make it obvious to Anna that she was looking for the mystery person. The tall figure she saw the other day could be anywhere in these woods. If it appeared again, she wanted to get a good look at him or her. Rebel walked uneasily behind Jett, breaking into a trot every time a branch cracked or the wind blew. Brynlei wondered who was more paranoid, Rebel or herself.

Anna was listing the ingredients of her favorite vegan stir-fry recipe when they reached the creek. Wild raspberries grew on thorny bushes next to it. This was the spot where they had stopped two days ago to let their horses take a drink. This was where she saw the figure dart behind the trees.

"Do you want to stop and let them drink?" Brynlei said.

"Sure."

Brynlei's eyes scanned the trees beyond the creek. No movement.

"Don't tell me you're looking for that person again." Anna tossed her head back. "You know it was just a deer, right?"

"Yeah. No. I mean, I'm just looking at all the trees." She was a horrible liar. Anna laughed.

"Yeah, right. You're even weirder than I thought. I like it."

After the horses quenched their thirst, they continued along the trail. Soon, light raindrops began to fall. Only a few made it through the trees to the girls and their horses, but the air was misty and wet.

"Well, that sucks," Anna said. "It's raining and we're still at least an hour from the barn."

Brynlei was about to say something about the trees sheltering them from the rain when Rebel bolted. For once, she didn't see it coming. Rebel spun sideways, grabbed the bit in his mouth, and galloped full-speed into the woods. Brynlei tried not to panic, even as she felt the thousand pinpricks of dark energy surround her. She sat back in the saddle and stretched tall, using her weight to try to slow Rebel down. She pulled as hard as she could on the reins. Rebel didn't respond to any of her efforts. He raced away from the trail and in between the trees, clearly terrified by some kind of monster he believed to be lurking in the woods. Rebel started to buck as he galloped. Brynlei felt completely out of control, like she was on roller coaster that had gone rogue.

The dark energy enveloped her, pressing in on her, suffocating her. She couldn't breathe. Something bad was going to happen. Rebel bucked again and knocked Brynlei into a low tree branch. The branch caught her in the stomach, jolted her feet out of the stirrups, and ripped the reins from her hands. She hung in the air before falling to the ground, as if in slow motion, then landed with a thud on the wet dirt. Brynlei lay still on the ground for a moment, making sure she was alive.

The fall had knocked the wind out of her and blurred her vision, but she could see. She could move her arms and legs. She sat up as Rebel galloped away, the reins from his bridle dangling dangerously down near his legs. A jolt of fear tore through her. There was so much that could go wrong. Rebel's reins could get caught on a tree branch or tangled up in his legs. Even if that didn't happen, Rebel could get lost in the woods. The last thing Brynlei wanted was for Rebel to hurt himself and she really didn't want to return to the barn without a horse. She had to find him as soon as possible.

Brynlei rose to her feet and took a shaky step. Something moved in the distance and she instinctively ran toward it. It had to be Rebel. However, as she searched between the trees for a better view, she saw Rebel wasn't alone. The shadowy figure of a girl stood next to him. Rebel now appeared calm, his reins draped safely back over his neck. Almost instantly, the girl disappeared from sight, darting into the thick cover of the forest. Brynlei started chasing after her.

"Wait!" She couldn't see the girl's face, but even through the thick mist and falling rain, she could see that the girl wore blue jeans and a faded gray T-shirt. Most importantly, long black hair flowed behind her as she ran. As quickly as she had appeared, the girl vanished.

The rain started to fall harder.

"Brynlei!" Anna's voice screeched from the distance in the other direction.

"Over here," Brynlei yelled.

Anna and Jett trotted through the trees toward Brynlei. Anna's eyes danced with fear, her face a picture of sheer panic.

"Are you okay?" Anna demanded.

"Yeah, I'm fine." As Brynlei said the words, the blood drained from her face and she felt sick. She didn't know if she should tell Anna what she had just seen. She wasn't sure Anna would believe her anyway.

"Oh, thank God. There's Rebel," Anna said, looking into the woods beyond Brynlei.

Sure enough, sticks and leaves crackled in the distance. Rebel was about a hundred yards away and walking toward them. He stopped and leisurely nibbled some leaves off a tree as if nothing had happened.

Anna hopped off Jett and handed his reins to Brynlei. She walked steadily toward Rebel and grasped the reins, which now lay safely back over the horse's neck.

"You're a freak, Rebel," Anna said as she led him back to Brynlei.

She was thankful that Anna took action so quickly. Brynlei had frozen. She knew what to do, but her arms and legs didn't respond. She stared off into the distance, searching for another glimpse of the girl.

"Are you sure you're okay?" Anna said again. "You look like you just saw a ghost."

Brynlei's hands shook as she clenched Jett's reins between her fingers. "I think I did."

"What?" Anna stopped.

Brynlei looked Anna straight in the eyes, struggling to hold back the tears. She couldn't handle this alone. She had to tell Anna. Anna was the only person at Foxwoode she trusted completely.

"You have to believe me," Brynlei said. "I just saw a girl running through the woods. She had long black hair. I think it was Caroline Watson."

Anna's mouth dropped open as she stared at Brynlei through her charcoal-lined eyes. Brynlei worried Anna would start laughing at her, or tell her that she must have hit her head too hard when she fell.

"How do you know?" Anna said,

"I couldn't see her face, but she had long black hair. That's exactly how people described Caroline Watson at the bonfire."

"But you think it's a ghost?" Anna's voice was a pitch higher now.

"I don't know. I mean she looked real, but she appeared of nowhere. I've seen ghosts before. At least, I think I have." Brynlei pictured her dead grandma sitting in the living room chair.

"I called to the girl, told her to wait, but then she just disappeared. It was hard to see through the rain and the trees."

Anna stared, stone-faced, drops of mist glistening on her nose ring.

"I don't know if she's real or not, but there's a girl out here in these woods. A girl who looks like Caroline Watson," Brynlei insisted. "Something happened to her four years ago. I need to find out what it was."

"I'm totally freaked out right now." Anna crossed her arms in front of her, as if hugging herself.

"Me too." No matter how hard Brynlei clenched her fists, she couldn't stop her hands from shaking

They decided to head back to the barn before Miss Jill sent out a search party. Anna offered to ride Rebel the rest of the way, but Brynlei insisted she could do it.

Just around a bend in the trail, they passed Bruce. He was on foot, trimming back stray branches that encroached onto the neatly groomed trail. He snipped and stacked the branches quickly, ignoring the rain. Did this guy ever stop working? Bruce nodded at them as they passed.

After he was safely out of earshot, Anna promised not to tell anyone about Brynlei's fall. They weren't sure if it would ruin Brynlei's chances of winning Top Rider, but they wouldn't risk it. Now they also had a second secret to keep. The one about the girl in the woods.

Chapter Nine

The next day, the weather cleared and the blazing sun shone relentlessly down on Foxwoode. Between the heat, her aching body, and the thoughts of Caroline Watson spinning through her mind, Brynlei barely made it through the morning riding lesson. Her stomach was sore from where the branch hit her, and the rest of her body throbbed from when she hit the ground.

Brynlei attempted to keep up with Miss Jill's demands, but when she asked Jett to canter he picked up the wrong lead, leading with his outside front leg instead of the inside front leg, causing them to be off balance. Four more times, Brynlei pulled Jett to a halt, slid her outside leg back, and gently felt Jett's mouth with her inside rein before asking for a canter on the correct lead. Each time, Jett lurched forward, awkwardly leading with his outside leg. On the fifth attempt, Jett picked up the correct lead and Brynlei exhaled deeply, thankful for the small victory. The lesson continued on its downhill slope. Brynlei struggled to find her distances to the jumps and, finally, went off course.

"Brynlei," Miss Jill shouted. "Focus. Do it again."

Brynlei guided Jett around the course again, still missing distances and leads. Her black helmet captured the heat like an oven baking her head. Sweat dripped into her eyes, blurring her vision. Brynlei couldn't concentrate. She felt like crying.

"What's going on with you today?" Miss Jill shook her head. "If you think this is hot, wait until this afternoon."

Alyssa snickered in the distance. On rare days like these Brynlei wondered why she couldn't be obsessed with a different sport, like swimming, volleyball, or golf. Some other sport that was enjoyable on a hot day and that didn't attract so many snobby girls.

After several long minutes, the lesson finally ended. Brynlei led Jett back to the barn and relieved him of the riding tack. She peeled off her helmet, gloves, and tall boots and slipped into her old tennis shoes. She and Jett were drenched in sweat. The other girls and horses didn't look much better. Jett walked willingly into one of the outdoor wash stalls, and Brynlei began spraying his legs with cool water. She carefully worked her way up his body so he had time to adjust to the temperature.

"Tough lesson," Anna said, leading Rebel into the wash stall next to Jett. "You doing okay?"

"Yeah." Brynlei lowered her voice to a whisper. "I mean, not really. I can't stop thinking about Caroline. We need to go back and find her."

"Not today. It's too hot and you need a break." Anna looked Brynlei up and down.

Brynlei let out a stifled laugh. She looked like a disaster.

"Anyway," Anna continued, "if Caroline, or her ghost, or whatever, has really been in the woods for the last four years, another day or two isn't going to make a difference."

"Yeah, okay, but you'll go back with me again, right?"

"Count on it." Anna winked. Then she picked up the hose and drenched Brynlei in a burst of freezing water.

* * * *

The Olsons canceled the afternoon ride because of the heat, so the girls flocked to the beach. The deep blue water of Lake Foxwoode remained surprisingly cool and provided relief when the heat became too oppressive. Brynlei lay motionless on her beach towel and let her back sink into the warm sand. She closed her eyes behind her oversize black sunglasses and tried to sleep. Unfortunately, Alyssa was only two beach towels away. Her incessant gossip pierced Brynlei's ears. Every time she began to drift off into relaxation, Alyssa's sharp voice slapped her in the face.

"Bryce, my boyfriend at home, is so adorable," Alyssa said. "He comes to my horse shows sometimes to watch me ride. He has no idea what I'm doing. He always says, 'Great job, Alyssa!' and then he hesitates and says, 'Was that great? I can't really tell the difference.'

Alyssa laughed loudly. McKenzie laughed too.

They had all heard way too much information about Bryce already. When Alyssa wasn't talking about her herd of show horses back in Chicago, she talked about Bryce. What kind of guy would see past Alyssa's fakeness? No one could argue she wasn't good-looking, but the guy would have to talk to her at some point. Wouldn't he be turned off then? Brynlei didn't get it.

Alyssa kept talking, "Bryce always used to wear these super hero T-shirts from Old Navy and I was like, if you want to wear those horrible T-shirts then you need to find a new girlfriend. So, I went to Nordstrom's with him and my dad's personal shopper helped him pick out a whole new wardrobe. I mean, he looks like a totally different person. I don't know why everyone doesn't shop at Nordstrom."

"I love Nordstrom," McKenzie said.

Brynlei wished she remembered to charge the battery on her iPod so she could drown out Alyssa's moronic remarks with her music.

"I think she was a Barbie doll in her past life," Anna muttered under her breath. Brynlei smiled.

"Bryce always used to wear brown and gray shirts, but I told him blue shirts bring out his eyes," Alyssa said. Colton Smith had worn a gray shirt the Saturday night of the party at Jessica Ralph's house.

Brynlei had admired Colton from afar at school for weeks by then. She looked forward to second period English and sixth period biology every day, just so she could be near him, so she could overhear his sarcastic comments, so she could catch a glimpse of his boyish smile and unbelievably blue eyes. They had only exchanged a few words to each other, but each time Colton spoke to her it was as if his words were electrically charged.

Brynlei had thought Colton was the one she wanted to be her boyfriend. She didn't care what color shirt he was wearing, or that his jeans were always ripped, or that he liked to talk about skateboarding. She had followed closely behind Rebecca as they walked into the party at Jessica's house with Rebecca serving as Brynlei's human shield. They found Colton standing in the kitchen drinking beer from a clear plastic cup. His ocean-blue eyes washed over Brynlei, pulling her into their tide.

"I didn't expect to see you here," Colton said, flashing his most enticing smile.

Brynlei forced herself to breathe. She tried to act cool, like she went to these parties all the time. Rebecca jabbed her with an elbow. No words came out.

"We thought we'd make a surprise appearance," Rebecca said, saving her. "I'm going to go find Jason." Rebecca left Brynlei and Colton alone in the corner of the kitchen. "I'll catch up with you in a while." Rebecca smiled and winked at her.

Rebecca was just trying to help her talk to Colton, but Brynlei wanted to scream at her, "Don't leave me! I can't do this on my own." Brynlei and Colton stood uncomfortably across from each other.

"Do you want a beer?" Colton asked.

"Okay," Brynlei said, although she really didn't want one. She didn't like the taste of beer and she promised her parents that she wouldn't drink if they let her go to parties. Yet she didn't want to say no to Colton. She didn't want him to think she was a dork.

Colton filled a cup from the keg and gave it to her. His fingers touched her hand as he passed her the cup and energy surged between them. She took a sip of the beer and pretended that it tasted good. Colton pointed to a long, red scrape on his left arm.

"I tried a new trick today. My board flew out from under me and I landed on my arm."

"Oh, my God," Brynlei said. "Did it hurt?"

"Not as much as the time when I broke my arm."

Their conversation flowed easily after that. Colton told stories of his skateboarding injuries and Brynlei described all of her riding injuries. Each time one of them rolled up a pant leg or lifted a shirt to reveal the body part where an injury had occurred, their imaginations filled in the blanks. Their attraction grew stronger.

"Do you want to go sit down somewhere?" Colton Finally said,

"Sure." She wasn't sure if that was code for something else, but if Colton Smith wanted to kiss her, she wasn't going to stop him. Colton grabbed her hand. Brynlei's beer was empty by then. It had gone down smoother with every sip. Her legs felt rubbery and her head floated, light and happy. Colton led her past some older students she didn't recognize and down a hall, opening doors and peering into each room.

"We can go in here," he finally said, pulling her into the home office of Jessica Ralph's unsuspecting parents.

"You're really pretty," Colton said, as he closed the door behind them and dimmed the lights. He slid his arms around her waist and pulled her close to him. Then he kissed her. It was a long, hard kiss, like he'd been thinking about it for weeks. When he finally came up for air, Brynlei leaned in and kissed him back. Another long, hard kiss. She didn't want it to end.

Colton was everything she wasn't. He was strong, funny, rugged, and cool. He smelled like cement, pepper, and beer. His gray, cotton T-shirt clung to his muscular body. She could have stayed there all night in his arms.

There was a loud knock on the door.

"Everybody out!" Jessica Ralph swung open the door. "Our neighbors called the police. You have to leave. Now!"

Brynlei and Colton walked out of the room into a crowd of students from Franklin Corners High. The bright lights in the hallway blinded her eyes and revealed her disheveled hair. Her face flushed. People looked at Colton and Brynlei and then at each other and smirked.

"Brynlei, come on. I've been looking all over for you," Rebecca said.

"Bye." Brynlei smiled at Colton.

"See you," Colton said.

Brynlei didn't know that would be the last time Colton talked to her. She was flying high after they left the party. She told Rebecca about their flirtatious conversation and the kiss that followed.

"Yeah, that was pretty obvious," Rebecca said. "You guys weren't very stealthy coming out of that room."

One of Jason's friends drove her home from the party before dropping Rebecca and Jason to their respective houses. Brynlei was home forty-five minutes before her curfew and slipped past her parents without arousing any suspicion. She couldn't believe that the boy she liked actually liked her back. She would finally have a boyfriend, just like Rebecca had Jason. She fell asleep happy that night.

On Sunday, Brynlei wondered if Colton would call or text her. She checked her phone every few minutes, but nothing. She called Rebecca to talk things through.

"He probably doesn't have your number," Rebecca assured her. "Besides, guys don't like to seem too eager. He's playing it cool."

"Yeah, I guess I didn't give him my number." Brynlei knew that Colton could have figured out a way to get her number if he really wanted to call her.

The next day, Brynlei spent extra time getting ready for school. She wanted to look like a knockout when Colton saw her again. She wore the jeans that Rebecca said made her butt look killer. She applied the mascara and lip-gloss that she often skipped. She wore the black shirt that made her eyes pop.

Brynlei first saw Colton as they walked into second period English. They almost ran into each other. She looked at Colton and began to smile, but Colton put his head down and walked into the classroom ahead of her. Brynlei almost dropped her notebook. She couldn't move. It was as if someone had punched her in the stomach. *Did he really just ignore me?* she wondered as students pushed their way past her to their seats.

The bell jolted her out of her head and she stumbled to her seat. She was thankful for the sturdy metal chair beneath her. Her legs would not have held out much longer. Colton sat a row ahead of her and one seat over, directly in her line of vision. She tried not to look at him.

Mrs. Davis, the English teacher, rambled on about the assignment they turned in on Friday, but Brynlei couldn't register the words coming out of Mrs. Davis' mouth. How could she have misjudged the situation with Colton so badly? How could she have thought that Colton actually liked her? Maybe he just didn't know what to say. Brynlei tried to give Colton the benefit of the doubt and make herself feel better at the same time. The harder she struggled to stare straight ahead, the more her eyes traveled to Colton. His sandy-brown hair and blue eyes were like a magnet pulling her eyes to him.

She studied him for any sign that he was thinking about her, for any sign that he felt bad about walking past her without even making eye contact. Colton sat in his chair and nodded along to whatever Mrs. Davis was saying. Colton wadded up a gum wrapper and flung it at Max, his buddy in the seat next to him.

"What the hell?" Max said to Colton, under his breath.

Colton shrugged his shoulders and laughed. He didn't have a care in the world.

Meanwhile, Brynlei struggled to keep the tears from welling up in her eyes. As the minutes ticked slowly by, she decided she would give Colton one more chance. She'd walk over to him as soon as class ended and ask how his arm was doing. Then maybe they'd joke about their injuries like they did on Saturday night, and everything would be back to the way she envisioned it.

When the bell rang, Brynlei leaned over to pick up her bag. She was ready to walk over to Colton. By the time she stood up, Colton's seat was empty. He had bolted out of the classroom and never even looked back.

* * * *

The next morning, the heat and humidity finally broke. A gentle breeze blew 75-degree air over Foxwoode and breathed new life into its inhabitants. The girls were up early and ready to ride. Brynlei, especially, was anxious to redeem herself after her disappointing ride the day before.

"Track left," Miss Jill shouted. "Pick up your posting trot."

The girls urged their horses forward, rising and falling in the saddle with each step.

"Kaitlyn, keep Daisey moving forward. Focus on pushing the horse from your leg into your hand," Miss Jill said. "You too, Alyssa. Bentley needs more impulsion. Get him on the bit and make him round."

Miss Jill continued critiquing their riding, one by one, as they trotted around the ring.

"Julia, bend Devon around your leg through the corner. Now everyone drop your stirrups."

A few groans escaped some of the Flying Foxes. Riding without stirrups was the quickest way to strengthen a rider's legs, but also the most strenuous of exercises.

"Try to get a little farther up out of the saddle, Brynlei," Miss Jill said. "Use the entire inside of your leg. Relax your knee."

Brynlei made the adjustments, so the next time she passed Miss Jill all she heard was, "Much better, Brynlei."

She noticed the other girls' positions as they rode. McKenzie seemed to be struggling. Her back was slouching, and she barely rose out of the saddle. Alyssa had a pained look on her face, but she kept up with Miss Jill's demands. Anna, however, looked as if she'd done this all her life. She never would have guessed Anna was riding without stirrups as she posted around the ring with her shoulders back, her hands quiet, and her legs in the perfect position. Anna's riding was impressive.

"Excellent, Anna," Miss Jill said every time Anna passed her.

They continued the lesson without stirrups.

"Change direction and pick up your right lead canter," Miss Jill instructed.

Brynlei's legs were burning, but she didn't dare complain. After another ten minutes of cantering, they were allowed to walk.

"We're going to be jumping without stirrups today," Miss Jill informed them matter-of-factly, as if she was inviting them to tea. "Walk your horses for five minutes and we'll start jumping the diagonal X. Julia, you'll go first."

Brynlei was suddenly thankful for all the times Terri made her ride without stirrups in her lessons at home. She had done this before, so she knew she could do it again.

One by one, they cantered toward the small jump set at an angle in the middle of the ring. Brynlei set a steady, forward pace so that she would find her distance. Sure enough, she and Jett sailed smoothly over the jump. All of the girls made it over, some prettier than others. They jumped the X again going in the other direction. Then Miss Jill set up a line of two low jumps.

"Now we'll do the outside line in five strides."

Julia went first and cantered out of the line in six strides.

"You need to ride it in a forward five," Miss Jill shouted.

Anna went next and nailed the line in five strides. Brynlei followed and also completed the line in five strides. Alyssa was the last to approach the line. Bentley cantered alarmingly fast as Alyssa turned him toward the line a second too late. Bentley barreled toward the first jump at an angle, and jumped it awkwardly. Then Alyssa legged Bentley forward and he bolted toward the second jump. Bentley left Alyssa behind as he leaped over the jump a half-stride early.

Without her stirrups, Alyssa couldn't hold on. She flew through the air like a rag doll before landing on the ground with a thud. All the girls watched in disbelief. For a fleeting moment, Brynlei felt bad for Alyssa. She must have been so embarrassed falling off her fancy horse in front of everyone. When Brynlei saw Anna's curved lips and sparkling eyes, she remembered that Alyssa didn't deserve her sympathy. Anna's face seemed to shout, "Hey everyone, we just saw Top Rider fall on her face." Brynlei hated that she found a hint of enjoyment in someone else's misery, but she was only human.

"Are you okay?" Miss Jill jogged toward Alyssa.

"Yes." Alyssa dusted herself off, as Bentley stared down at his lost rider. "Stupid Bentley. He jumped before I asked him."

"That wasn't Bentley's fault." Miss Jill's voice was sharper than a butcher knife. "Your approach to the line was crooked and it snowballed from there. Get back on and do it again."

Although Alyssa rode the line almost perfectly the second time, the damage had been done. There was a chink in Alyssa's Top Rider armor.

Chapter Ten

The next afternoon, Brynlei lugged her overflowing basket to the laundry cabin at the bottom of the hill. After a checkered sleep the night before, she decided her sheets and towels could use a wash. The grains of sand on her sheets had rubbed against her arms and legs like sandpaper, keeping her awake for much of the night. No matter which way she flipped and turned, she could not get comfortable with the tiny pebbles scratching her skin.

As she'd lain in bed, wishing for sleep, Brynlei's mind drifted toward home. She wondered if Rebecca was having fun at Interlochen. Surely, Rebecca would be wowing everyone there with her musical abilities and her comedic impersonations. Brynlei's chest felt as if it was collapsing in upon itself when she thought of how much she missed her closest friend. She wished she could talk to Rebecca. She yearned to tell her everything that was happening at Foxwoode. Her story would sound crazy and unbelievable, but she would tell Rebecca every detail. She'd tell her about the ghost story of Caroline Watson and of seeing the girl in the woods. She'd tell her about Alyssa, Anna, Miss Jill, Bruce, Debbie, and Jett. Rebecca would listen and help her as only Rebecca could. Brynlei's only way to make a call was through the landline in the office and she wouldn't risk having anyone overhear her. Besides, Rebecca was busy on her own summer adventure. Brynlei would have to wait to confide in her friend.

She realized she hadn't called her mom and dad yet. She needed to do that. They were probably anxious to hear from her, so she made a mental note to call them after dinner. Of course, Brynlei wouldn't tell them about the girl in the woods even if she were able to make a private phone call. Their conversation would stay safely on the surface, as it always did. They'd throw out their life-preserver topic of weather, food, or sports, making sure the discussion never went too deep. She could tell them about the horses and the girls and the food in the mess hall. She could tell Mom that she'd washed her sheets and towels, as instructed. Hearing their familiar voices would give her a boost.

To Brynlei's relief, all of the washing machines were available. She slid the quarters into the first washing machine and loaded the sheets and towels, shaking out the excess sand first. Despite the wide selection of magazines hanging on the wall and the comfortable sitting area, the thought of waiting in the laundry cabin for the cycle to complete was unbearable. The pungent smell of laundry detergent clogged her nose and the spinning motor of the washing machine whirred in her ears.

She'd use her free time to visit the horses and give Jett's mane and tail a good brushing. She stepped out into the fresh air and began walking toward the barn. Footsteps shuffled closely behind her. She turned around and faced Bruce, who stood next to the laundry cabin door. Their eyes locked for a split second before he looked down and shuffled through the door. It was odd, though. He wasn't carrying any dirty clothes with him. Maybe he was going in there to do repairs on one of the machines. Except he wasn't carrying any tools either. She couldn't shake the unsettling feeling that Bruce had followed her. That didn't make sense, though. Why would he be following her? Brynlei had no idea. One thing she did know was that her gut instincts were almost always right.

* * * *

Jett stood quietly in the grooming stall as Brynlei fed him treats and ran her hands over his velvety face. Few things calmed her more than a horse's breath on her face—each warm burst of air pumped renewed energy directly into her soul. Jett seemed to be enjoying every second of the extra attention being showered on him. Every time Brynlei stopped petting him, Jett lowered his head and nuzzled her or nibbled at her shirt. She loved the way horses didn't know their own strength; Jett's friendly nuzzles almost knocking her off her feet.

Like every other horse she'd ever encountered, Jett's large brown eyes were all-knowing. She'd always thought that horses' eyes were like two crystal balls that could see the past, present, and future all at once. She'd read much about the collective unconsciousness of horses, and had no doubt horses remembered their past lives as well as the past lives of all other horses. In Brynlei's opinion, this made horses much wiser than humans, although it pained her that Jett could feel the terror of all the horses that had been mistreated by humans throughout history, sacrificed in wars, abused by harsh training methods, and neglected by careless owners. She believed past events influenced the behavior of all living horses and explained behavioral problems in horses that had never been mistreated at all. On the bright side, she knew she could make a difference by contributing positive energy to the collective unconsciousness of horses. Every act of kindness, no matter how small, tipped the scales toward happiness and understanding.

Brynlei knew better than to share her insights on collective unconsciousness with others. The one time she'd tried to explain the idea to some girls in her riding group at home, she'd been mocked. She'd been around long enough to know most people saw things in black and white. Trying to convince people to believe in something they could not see at all was a fruitless effort. People wanted proof, something they could hold in their hands.

Brynlei was different from most people. She trusted her feelings and her instincts more than scientific studies. Connecting the dots was never a problem.

She applied a dab of mane-and-tail conditioner to Jett's long tail and combed gently through the tangles. Although Jett wasn't her horse, she would treat him as if he were for these three weeks. He deserved to be loved and pampered as much as any privately-owned horse. She could do that for him. Brynlei remembered her laundry in the washing machine and realized it was time to move it to the dryer, but she wasn't ready to leave yet. She and Jett were the only ones in the barn, and it was peaceful. She pressed her face against Jett's soft neck and then rubbed his ears. She studied the depths of Jett's eyes and wondered what else he knew.

* * * *

After lunch the next day, the girls of Cabin 5 headed to the beach to relax for a couple hours before the afternoon free ride. Brynlei didn't follow them. She wanted to stay in the cabin and read her book. After a week of solid activity, Foxwoode's schedule was wearing her out. She needed some time to herself. Brynlei hoped Anna would stay back, too, so they could talk about their plan for finding Caroline Watson or the ghost of Caroline Watson. She still wasn't sure what she had seen. Anna said she wanted to lie on the beach and listen to music. Anna must have seen the disappointment in Brynlei's eyes.

"We'll talk about it tonight," she whispered to Brynlei as she left the cabin. "Don't do anything stupid without me."

Brynlei changed into clean clothes and lay on her bunk. She stared at the neat wooden slats holding up the bed above hers and relished the silence. Her clean sheets were free of sand, but were no longer tight around her ankles. She lacked her mom's ability to make crisp hospital corners.

A wave of homesickness washed over her. She missed everything— her brother and Maverick, the privacy of her bedroom, Rebecca, and, most of all, her parents. Her phone call with them last night had been brief. She'd had enough time to reassure them she was having a great time and making friends. She told them about Jett and Miss Jill and Anna. Her parents seemed genuinely elated to hear from her, but they explained they were late for a dinner at their neighbor's house. So, after just a few minutes of talking, Brynlei hung up and felt like she hadn't really told them anything.

She wondered if her mom was baking something right now. Her mom was almost always creating something delicious. Her baking had always been a fun hobby, but it quickly became something more. When her mom had started giving her unique concoctions to friends as gifts, they begged for more. Then they offered to pay. Soon after, her mom started taking orders online.

Jackie Leighton's baked goods were no run-of-the-mill chocolate chip cookies and blueberry muffins. She baked chocolate-peppermint muffins and tomato-cilantro bread. Her lemon-lavender scones were her best seller. Brynlei's favorite was her mom's salted caramel and coconut cookies. What she wouldn't do for one chewy bite of one of those cookies. Not that the food at Foxwoode was bad. It was actually very good, but it didn't taste like home.

Her mom's dream was to open her own bakery on a main street of some quaint town, but reality kept her dream at bay. For the past few years, her mom had spent most of her time shuttling Brynlei and her brother between school, baseball practice, and horseback riding lessons. When she'd asked her mom about opening her own bakery once, her mom surprised her.

"Sometimes dreams are better left as dreams." Her mom had smiled and gazed out the front windshield as she drove. "I like my life the way it is. I'm happy just to have the dream."

Brynlei longed to be content like her mom. Her life would be so much easier if she didn't always feel the need to reach the next goal and accomplish the next task. Like a hoarder who collects more and more junk without realizing that the stuff doesn't fill the hole, Brynlei always wanted more. Not more stuff, just more. Why couldn't she be satisfied that she was finally at Foxwoode? Why did she need to be Top Rider? Why did she feel compelled to identify the mysterious figure in the woods? Brynlei wished she could leave it alone, but she couldn't.

Her thoughts screeched to a halt. The air had an electric charge, as if a thunderstorm was forming outside her window. The hairs on the back of her neck stood on end. There was movement in the hallway. A creaking sound and some shuffling and then another groan of a floorboard. Someone was in the cabin.

"Anna?" Brynlei called. Complete silence followed. "Is someone there?" The words barely formed in her dry mouth.

Brynlei remembered the lights that had mysteriously turned on and off in the bathroom. She pulled her legs out from under the covers. Another creak came from the hallway. Her feet fumbled into the flip-flops that lay on the floor. She wanted to know who was in their cabin and why they were being so secretive about it.

Rushing to the hallway, Brynlei rounded the corner, practically running. She stopped dead in her tracks. No one was there. The bathroom was empty too. Suddenly, the whole cabin felt eerily desolate. Confused and flustered, she burst through the screen door and ran outside. She was desperate for air. Maybe she really was going crazy.

Maybe her imagination was running away with her after all.

"You okay?" Bruce said.

Brynlei jumped. She hadn't seen him standing behind the bushes. There was a hint of anger in Bruce's eyes that she hadn't noticed before. Maybe Brynlei's instincts about Bruce had been wrong. Maybe the other girls were right about him.

"Yeah. I guess. I thought I heard someone in the cabin, but then there was no one there." Brynlei struggled to suck in air.

"Probably heard me trimmin' the bushes," Bruce said. "You should be at the beach with the other girls."

An unsettling feeling spread through her, as her warm blood turned cold. Although Bruce had not outwardly threatened her, she felt intimidated by the tone of his voice and the accusatory look in his eyes.

"I was just leaving."

She took off running toward the beach, not bothering to go back for her bathing suit or towel.

* * * *

Brynlei slowed to a walk and made her way down the narrow dirt pathway through the patch of woods that led to the beach. The girls of Cabin 5 lay motionless on their beach towels like beached whales. She inhaled deeply through her mouth and exhaled through her nose to slow her pounding heart as she approached the girls, pretending to be in control of her own body.

"Did you forget something?" Alyssa asked, unplugging an ear bud and looking at Brynlei's clothes.

"Oh, I just thought I'd see what you guys are up to." Brynlei had not thought out her story in advance. It wouldn't make sense to tell the truth. After all, nothing had really happened, but there was safety in numbers.

"Sit down." Anna's blue hair was slicked back and dripping with lake water. "You can have half of my towel." Anna smoothed out the oversized beach towel and Brynlei sat on the edge, digging her toes into the warm sand. The girls lay silently, each plugged into her own iPod, each escaping into her own musical world.

Brynlei sat and stared out at Lake Foxwoode. The sun reflecting off the surface of the lake burned her eyes. The blinding glare was like a shield protecting everything that lay beneath the silent water. The woods beyond the lake formed a dense and dark wall. Each tree stood its ground, like soldiers in an army protecting the secrets that lay within the vast expanse beyond.

Scanning the trees for any sign of movement, Brynlei knew there was a girl, dead or alive, that roamed beyond the fortress of trees. She was becoming more and more certain the figure she saw running in the woods was that of Caroline Watson. Perhaps the ghost story that Alyssa told the first night at the bonfire was true. Perhaps Caroline was murdered and could not rest in peace until the person or people who killed her were brought to justice.

Brynlei now wondered if Bruce was, in fact, involved in Caroline's death. She had no proof, of course, but she had seen a different side of Bruce today. A side that frightened her. How could she have misjudged his character so badly? She could usually sense the energy emanating from people immediately. Her initial instincts were rarely wrong.

Then again, she had been horribly wrong about Colton Smith. Or maybe Bruce had nothing to do with Caroline. The girl could have been killed by the jealous girls in her cabin. Could they have followed her into the woods and attacked her? Maybe it was a prank that got out of control. An accident. Maybe not. It didn't make sense that an experienced rider like Caroline would leave on a trail ride by herself, not wearing a helmet. On top of that, Caroline surely would have known to check the girth to make sure it was tight before mounting her horse. That was Horsemanship 101.

Brynlei needed to find out what had really happened to Caroline. The thoughts swarmed in her head like mosquitoes to warm flesh on a humid day. She had to do something more than just shoe the mosquitoes away. She needed to squash them.

When Brynlei was sure the other girls were completely absorbed in their music, she nudged Anna. Anna sat up with a start.

"I was almost asleep." Anna squinted her eyes at Brynlei. "Is time to go?"

Brynlei placed her finger on her lips.

"Shh." She looked at the other girls to make sure they weren't paying attention. They were sprawled in a row like zombies, lost in their own worlds.

"I have to tell you something," Brynlei whispered. "We need to go back into the woods today, during free ride."

"Fine," Anna said, closing her eyes. "I already told you I would go. Can I go back to sleep?"

"No. There's something else," Brynlei continued in a hushed tone. "I think Bruce came into our cabin when I was in my bunk a few minutes ago. I heard footsteps in the hallway, but no one was there. He was standing outside when I ran out the door." Brynlei couldn't get the words out of her mouth fast enough. "He seemed angry, almost like he was threatening me. That's why I ran straight here."

"What did he say to you?" Anna opened her eyes wide now.

"He said, 'You should be at the beach with the other girls.'" Brynlei did her best impersonation of Bruce's angry voice. Anna laughed.

"Is that really what he sounded like? That doesn't sound very threatening."

"I'm not good at imitations, but it was creepy. I was thinking, maybe Alyssa was right. Maybe Bruce was involved in Caroline Watson's disappearance."

"Woah," Anna said. "Jump to any conclusions lately? Bruce was probably just having a bad day and he got a little snippy with you. His job pretty much sucks. Cut him some slack."

"Okay." Brynlei could not forget the icy glare in Bruce's eyes. "Let's just ride as far into the woods as we can today and see what we can figure out."

"Sounds good. *Now* can I go back to sleep?" Anna said.

"Yes." Brynlei sat on the edge of Anna's towel and searched the trees for any sign of Caroline. Forty-five minutes later, it was time to get ready for free riding.

* * * *

This time they rode their own horses. Brynlei and Jett led the way along the narrow dirt path through the crowded trees. They decided to follow the Blue trail again; at least that's what they wrote on the clipboard in the barn. However, their plan was to take a detour when they reached the spot where Brynlei had seen the girl running. The air felt heavier today. There was no discussion of quirky horses, past lives, or recipes—only their mission to discover the truth about Caroline.

"Do you believe that I saw her?" Brynlei asked Anna when they reached a resting spot.

"Yes. I'm the only one crazy enough to believe you."

"Do you think it was an accident? Like her horse spooked and she hit her head on a rock and fell into the river. Or do you think someone murdered her? The other girls could have been jealous of her because she was going to win Top Rider and she was so pretty. Or it could have been Bruce," Brynlei added with some hesitation.

"I don't know, but there must have been something sketchy going on because they never found her body," Anna said. "Someone covered up the evidence."

"I guess it's possible that she's still alive." Brynlei shrugged. "Maybe she was running from something."

"Not likely." Anna shook her head. "Do you know how cold it gets up here in the winter? What would she eat? There's no way."

"Maybe someone kidnapped her," Brynlei said.

"She would have escaped by now. All she'd have to do is run over to the camp. It's been four years."

"I've heard that sometimes kidnappers brainwash their victims so that they become loyal to the people who took them. Maybe it's something like that." Brynlei stroked the velvety fur on Jett's neck as she spoke.

"I doubt it," Anna replied.

"I'm just trying to think of all the possibilities."

"We should do some research. Get the facts." Anna's eyes brightened. "There's a computer in the office. We can sneak in when no one's there."

"I wish I had reception on my phone." Brynlei stared up at the open sky, as if a cell phone tower might magically appear.

"Me, too. That's not gonna happen way out here."

The girls resumed their journey, asking their horses to trot in order to cover more ground. After another thirty minutes or so, they came to the spot where Rebel had bolted off the trail carrying Brynlei with him. She broke out in a cold sweat as she urged Jett off the trail and cut directly into the thick brush. Anna didn't say a word. She and Rebel followed loyally.

They were breaking Foxwoode's rules by going off the marked trail. They could get kicked out for this. Even worse, if anything happened to them, no one would know where they were. While Anna may have broken quite a few rules in her life, Brynlei had not. She'd never colored outside the lines, skipped a class, or cheated on a test. Something was different this time. It was as if an external force was pulling her off the trail and into the woods. She didn't have a choice.

As they made their own path, the space between the trees opened, making it easier to find a clear route. Brynlei's uneasiness grew with each step Jett took. The dark energy prickled her skin. Her flesh tingled, taking on a life of its own. This hyper-alert feeling was becoming all too familiar. Every twig that broke under the horses hooves sounded like a firecracker in her ears. She heard rustling in the distance. Not the rustling of the wind in the trees. This rustling had a different texture to it. She could feel the distinctive pressure on her body of someone watching her.

"Do you see anything?" she whispered back to Anna.

"No. Not yet," Anna replied.

"Someone's watching us."

Brynlei looked back at Anna and saw, for the first time, the look of fear in Anna's eyes. She hadn't meant to scare Anna, but the truth was that Brynlei was scared, too.

They continued, searching for any sign, any clue of what could have happened to Caroline. Brynlei heard it before she saw it, the rustling noise again. Now it was much closer. Something bounded through the trees, heading directly toward them. Rebel reared up as Ranger darted in between the two horses and barked loudly.

"Ranger, what the—" began Anna.

A second later, Bruce emerged from the trees.

"Ranger, come," Bruce shouted. Bruce stopped in front of Rebel, taking in the girls, his fists clenched. "You ain't allowed out here. You're off the trail."

Brynlei did not know what to do or say. She froze in fear.

"We must have taken a wrong turn," Anna said. Once again, Brynlei was thankful for Anna's quick thinking.

Bruce stared into Anna's eyes for a second too long, as if he knew she was lying.

"Were you following us?" Brynlei demanded. She could not believe the words that just came out of her mouth. She wished she could take them back.

"No. I'm teachin' Ranger to be a huntin' dog. Figured he was trackin' something. Follow me back to the trail," Bruce said.

Bruce turned around and walked ahead of Rebel. He retraced their makeshift path back toward the Blue trail. They probably walked for ten minutes, but it seemed like time was standing still. No one dared to talk. It was obvious now as they made their way over the rugged brush and back onto the freshly-groomed trail that Bruce knew they were lying about taking a wrong turn. The silence grew more awkward with each step.

When they were back on the Blue trail, Bruce stood in front of them blocking their path. "Why don't you tell me what you're really doin' out here?"

Brynlei held her breath and waited to see what Anna would say. She hoped Anna wouldn't reveal their secret. A thick curtain of silence hung between them.

"Like I said, we took a wrong turn," Anna finally said, not flinching. Brynlei exhaled.

"Don't go off the trail again. It ain't safe." Bruce's threatening tone revealed itself again. He stepped out of the way, but his pale blue eyes bore into them as they passed.

Anna dug her heel into Rebel's side and took off at a gallop. Brynlei followed. They had just escaped something, although she wasn't sure what.

* * * *

After they put their horses away, Brynlei and Anna walked back to their cabin. The sun sat low in the sky. Dinner would be starting soon.

"Do you think he followed us?" Brynlei looked over her shoulder to see if Bruce was anywhere in the vicinity.

"Yes," Anna said. "You were right. He's hiding something."

"We must have been heading in the right direction."

"Listen, Brynlei. I know you have your heart set on solving this mystery, or whatever you think it is, and I want to know the truth about Caroline Watson, too, but I don't want to get sent home." Anna hesitated. "Or murdered."

Brynlei's heart skipped a beat. She needed Anna's help. Brynlei couldn't speak.

"Let's just lay low for a while," Anna said.

Brynlei felt herself deflating. They still had almost two weeks to figure out what happened to Caroline. She could let it rest for a day or two.

"Okay." Brynlei stepped in front of Anna. "We should do the research though. On the computer. No one will know what we're doing."

"Wow. You are relentless," Anna shook her head. "I'm going to start calling you Nancy Drew."

They laughed as they entered their cabin, understanding that neither of them would tell anyone about their afternoon.

* * * *

The next morning, the girls groomed their horses in preparation for the morning lesson. Brynlei tried to do everything in her power to avoid Bruce, but he seemed to be lurking around every corner. He walked past the grooming stall where she tacked up Jett. He began to sweep the barn aisles, not making eye contact with anyone. To everyone else, he was probably invisible. Yet Brynlei could only see him, as much as she tried to avoid it. He was like the mind-bender picture Rebecca had shown her last year. The picture looked like a princess until Brynlei stared at it for a really long time. Then somehow, the picture transformed into a witch. She could never look at the picture again without seeing the witch.

One of the part-time barn hands drove a tractor full of hay past the open barn door, casting a long shadow down the aisle. The other girls talked and laughed, but Brynlei kept to herself. She wanted to get out to the ring and away from Bruce as quickly as possible.

Brynlei pulled on her riding gloves and tightly gripped the braided reins. She led Jett down the aisle, past Bruce, and out toward Ring A, where Miss Jill was walking the distance between two jumps. Anna strained to tighten Rebel's girth at the edge of the ring.

"Looks like a brutal course today," Anna said as Brynlei

91

approached.

Before Brynlei could answer, Miss Jill interrupted. "Girls, now that you're both here, we need to talk." The tone of her voice indicated she was not joking around. "Get on your horses and meet me in the middle of the ring."

Brynlei's stomach lurched into her throat. She couldn't believe she was in trouble, especially at Foxwoode. Bruce must have reported them. Brynlei and Anna did as they were told and rode to the middle of the ring, out of earshot of the other girls.

"You've both been reported as breaking one of Foxwoode's most important rules. You must ALWAYS, ALWAYS stay on the trails. There are no exceptions. This is for your own safety. If you are off the trail and something happens to you, we have no way to find you."

"We took a wrong turn," Anna said, sticking to her story.

"I find that difficult to believe," Miss Jill said, calling her bluff. "The trails are expertly groomed and very well-marked. Now, do you understand that this is your first and only warning?"

"Yes," Brynlei and Anna said at the same time.

Brynlei knew what was coming next. After all, she had read the Foxwoode Code of Conduct about a hundred times after memorizing the brochure.

"You only receive one warning after breaking a rule. The second time you break a rule, the Olsons will send you home. Please don't let that happen." Miss Jill stared directly into their eyes.

"We won't," Anna said, speaking for both of them.

"Now get out to the rail and pick up your posting trot," Miss Jill said, attempting to put the episode behind them.

Chapter Eleven

That Wednesday night, Foxwoode scheduled a bowling outing for the girls. Cabin 5 buzzed with excitement. After ten days of living in the semi-wilderness, they were eager to get a taste of civilization, if only for a few hours. Alyssa made a big show of laying out all of her potential outfits and making sure everyone knew which designer label marked each shirt, skirt, pair of shoes, and purse. Julia and McKenzie struggled to choose their outfits as well. There was a cute yellow sundress, a pair of skinny jeans, halter-tops in various colors, and a selection of skirts. Brynlei was thankful when Kaitlyn brought them all back to reality.

"Seriously, guys? We're going bowling. This isn't a red carpet event."

"There were boys from the hockey camp at the bowling alley last year. HOT boys." Alyssa tossed her hair over her shoulder. "Last year I wasn't prepared."

"Don't you have a boyfriend?" Anna said.

Alyssa held up a sequined mini-skirt, ignoring the question.

Brynlei had packed very few non-riding clothes that were suitable for an evening out. However, she did know from page five of the Foxwoode brochure that a trip to the bowling alley was a possibility. She pulled on her favorite jeans and a black V-neck T-shirt that fit her in such a way to show off what few curves she had. Then she put on her favorite hoop earrings. That was about as dressed up as she ever got. Anna also did not seem to have any problem choosing her outfit— tattered jeans, flip-flops, and a blue graphic tee that said *Going Back to Cali* in aqua letters. The lettering accentuated the blueness of her hair.

"From Old Navy," she whispered to Brynlei, smiling.

93

"Nice of you to get dressed up, Anna," Alyssa said. Alyssa had a way of insulting people that was vague enough to prevent the person who was being insulted from fighting back.

She had ultimately decided on wearing the tight pink mini-skirt with the white-sequined tank top and high-heeled sandals. She would look ridiculous in the bowling alley.

"We're going bowling," Anna said. "Not clubbing in Vegas."

Despite the clothing drama, Brynlei was thankful to have a distraction from whatever secret taunted her from the woods. She and Anna had been on the straight and narrow for the last three days, terrified of being sent home. She planned to talk to Anna tonight about their next step.

Brynlei choked on the diesel fumes and dust, as a yellow school bus lurched to a halt outside the mess hall at five. Miss Jill and Miss Ashley ushered the girls on board, instructing them to fill the seats row by row. Brynlei's mouth filled with saliva, the smell of the bus making her nauseous. It amazed her that all buses, no matter where they were found, smelled exactly the same—a chemical-laden swirl of burnt rubber tires, cheap pleather seats, and clouds of diesel.

Brynlei and Anna found themselves in the seat across from Alyssa and McKenzie. She hoped the loud motor of the bus's engine would drown out Alyssa's whiny voice, but it seemed even the rumbling mass of steel and gasoline was no match for Alyssa's piercing laugh. The bus started down the long dirt road, bouncing past the cabins, the pastures, and the woods until finally reaching Foxwoode's impressive gated entrance at the main road. Someone had left the gate open for the bus to pass through. The gate was usually kept closed and locked in order to keep the undesirables out. Or perhaps to keep secrets in.

"We have to look up information on Caroline's disappearance," Brynlei said under her breath, once the bus traveled farther down the two-lane highway. She expected resistance from Anna.

"We can do it tomorrow," Anna said. "When everyone is at breakfast. I was late for breakfast this morning. I looked in the office. No one was there and the door was open."

"Okay."

A surge of adrenaline rushed through Brynlei. There had to be more information about Caroline out there. Even a news article could help put some of the pieces of the puzzle in place.

"Now, don't think about it anymore," Anna said, as if she knew Brynlei was ruminating on the subject already. "We're supposed to be having fun."

Thirty minutes later, the bus pulled into the parking lot of a bowling alley on the outskirts of a one-stoplight town. The bowling alley appeared to have been lost in time, preserved from the 1950s or 60s. the letter *L* light was burnt out on the neon sign in front, causing the sign to flash *BOW ING.*

"Awesome!" Anna said, when she saw the outside of the building.

The parking lot contained a smattering of cars and two other buses parked in the far corner. Nervous chatter and laughter filled the bus.

"Attention, ladies," Miss Jill shouted from the front of the bus. "Everyone gets four tickets. Each ticket will buy you a round of bowling. Pizza and pop will be served at our reserved tables at six thirty. The bus will leave promptly at nine. I don't need to remind you there will be absolutely no drinking of alcohol allowed. Miss Ashley and I will be inside with you if you have any questions."

As the girls left the bus, Miss Jill handed them their tickets.

"Have fun. Have fun," she repeated to each girl that passed.

Brynlei's heart beat rapidly as she forced herself through the doors of the bowling alley. The bright lights in the entryway blinded her eyes. Bowling pins crashed like thunder. A group of men cheered. Bowling balls banged against the wooden floors. She needed to stand still for a moment to adjust to the brashness of her new surroundings. People stared as the boisterous group of girls clamored through the doors. She tried to stand behind Anna, to blend into the group. Anything not to draw attention to her while she felt so vulnerable.

Brynlei followed closely behind Anna as they made their way to the shoe counter.

"Oh, my God," Alyssa shrieked. "Look at how ugly these shoes are!" She cackled and McKenzie's laughter followed.

"I wouldn't be caught dead in those." Alyssa doubled over in laughter.

A middle age woman with thick glasses and graying hair stood behind the shoe counter. She observed Alyssa, with her bleached blonde hair and designer clothes, as if she had never seen anyone like her, as if she couldn't even comprehend what planet Alyssa had just flown in from. A flash of embarrassment or shame flickered in the woman's eyes.

Brynlei imagined the woman was asking herself how she got to this point, serving a group of spoiled, teenage girls in a bowling alley in the middle of nowhere.

"I'll take a size eight," Anna said, pushing Alyssa aside.

"I'll take a seven," Brynlei said. She wanted the woman to know that they weren't like Alyssa.

"Here you go, girls." The woman handed over two pairs of battered shoes.

"Thank you." Brynlei's voice was a little too loud and she made a point of looking the woman straight in the eyes when she said it.

Kaitlyn and Julia moved up to the counter to get their shoes. Kaitlyn told the other girls that she and Julia went bowling on occasion "just for fun" in Grand Rapids. They were used to bowling shoes.

"Seriously. It's no big deal," Kaitlyn said.

Brynlei followed Anna to an open lane near one end of the bowling alley. A group of teenage boys filled the lane to their right, laughing and taunting each other. Two of them wore black T-shirts that said *North Woods Hockey Camp*. Brynlei tried not to look at them. She struggled to breathe deeply and play it cool, which she knew was not her strong suit. Anna waved Kaitlyn and Julia over to their lane.

"I can't even be around her," Anna said, nodding her head toward Alyssa. "She's an embarrassment."

"She's just Alyssa," Julia said, not exactly defending her.

"She's out of touch and offensive." Anna wasn't backing down.

Brynlei wished Anna wouldn't say anything else about Alyssa in front of Kaitlyn and Julia. They were friends with Alyssa and chances were that any negative comments Anna made would make it back to Alyssa in some form or another.

"Should we start bowling?" Brynlei said, hoping to change the direction of the conversation.

"Sure," Julia said. "Me and Kaitlyn versus you and Anna."

"I've only bowled once before," Brynlei said. "It didn't go so well."

"Why do I have the feeling we're going to get our asses kicked?" Anna smirked.

Brynlei laughed.

Kaitlyn bowled first and threw a strike. She jumped up and down, her red hair bouncing. Julia's turn was equally impressive. Anna threw a gutter ball, but then knocked down five pins on her second try. On Brynlei's first attempt, the bowling ball slipped out of her fingers, landed with a deafening clank, and then rolled sideways into the gutter.

"Nice," Anna said.

The loud thud of the bowling ball drew the attention of the boys in the next lane.

"Can you do that again?" one of the boys said. "That was awesome." Laughter from the other boys followed.

"I don't think that can be duplicated," Anna replied.

Brynlei wanted to prove to everyone that she could do this. She prepared for her next throw, stepping forward, swinging the ball under, and releasing. This time the ball stuck to her fingers instead of gliding down the lane, as she envisioned. The ball fell straight down with a loud bang, landing on Brynlei's toe.

"Ouch." She hopped up and down.

More laughter from the boys.

"Hey, Cali," said the same boy. He was talking to Anna, referring to her "Going Back to Cali" T-shirt. "Can I give your friend some pointers?"

"My name's Anna, and, yes, please give her some pointers."

The boy walked over. He was tall with short dark hair and mahogany eyes that twinkled. His boyish smile was unexpected and disarming.

"Hey." He smiled at Brynlei. "I'm Luke."

"Hi." Luke's smile paralyzed Brynlei.

"Do you have a name?"

"Oh, yeah." Brynlei had temporarily forgotten how to speak. "I mean, I'm Brynlei."

"Okay, so when you take the ball back, try to square up so you're facing down the center of the lane. Then turn your palm forward when you release," Luke explained.

"Don't listen to him," one of the other boys shouted. "He sucks at bowling." More laughter.

"Here, let me show you." Luke took the bowling ball. Demonstrating the correct form, he threw the ball down the lane. Just before reaching the pins, it veered off to the right into the gutter. Waves of laughter erupted from his friends. Brynlei laughed, too.

"Maybe there's something wrong with this ball," Brynlei said.

"Yeah, that's probably it." Luke winked at her. "Let me know if you need any more help." He walked a few steps back over to his friends.

After that, the ice was broken. The girls continued with their game and the boys stopped by every few minutes to crack a joke or ask them questions.

Brynlei was in disbelief that someone like Luke seemed to be interested in her. She was jittery, afraid of saying the wrong thing. He made her stomach feel sick. Not like the bus. This was a good kind of sick, kind of like the way she felt before a horse show. Luke made it easy. Their conversation was effortless. They talked about hockey, horses, and bowling.

Before long, Alyssa and McKenzie wandered over, looking out of place in their high-heeled sandals.

"Like moths to a flame," Anna said under her breath.

It took exactly two seconds for Alyssa to insert herself in the conversation.

"Weren't you guys here last summer?" she said, flipping her blonde hair over her shoulder. Before anyone could answer, she looked at Luke and said, "I remember you."

Flames ignited inside Brynlei. She wanted to shout, "Get away from him, Alyssa. He's too good for you. He can see right through your fakeness. Besides, you already have a boyfriend at home." Instead, Brynlei stood by silently, watching Alyssa flirt with Luke. She knew she couldn't compete with Alyssa's innate confidence and Barbie doll looks.

"Yeah, this is our hang-out spot when we're at hockey camp." Luke's eyes traveled to Brynlei as he talked.

"I guess we should come here more often." Alyssa giggled.

Just as Brynlei thought she was going to be steam-rolled by Alyssa, Luke turned his back on Alyssa and faced her.

"Brynlei, we just finished a game. Do you want to be on my team for the next round?"

It took Brynlei a moment to realize what Luke had just asked her. She wasn't sure who was more stunned, Alyssa or herself.

"Sure," Brynlei said, finally able to spit out the word that was stuck in her throat.

She walked over to the boys' lane without looking back. Brynlei didn't need to look back. She could feel the fury emanating from Alyssa and clawing at her back. Brynlei glanced sideways at Anna, who smiled and gave her an approving nod.

"We need a fourth," yelled a boy named Jacob. "Cali, get over here."

Two other boys, William and Lance, paired up with Julia and Kaitlyn in the girls' lane. Alyssa and McKenzie lingered with them, but they were spectators, not participants.

"We're going to get some pizza," McKenzie said at one point. Brynlei felt bad for McKenzie and wondered why she remained so loyal to her horrible friend.

"Ugh! It's only seven," Alyssa complained. "We have two more hours of this."

"She seems high-maintenance," Luke said, looking at Alyssa as she walked away.

At that moment, Brynlei wanted more than anything to kiss Luke.

"She is." She couldn't stop the smile from spreading across her face.

The next two hours were the fastest of her life. She couldn't believe it when Miss Jill's voice came over the loud speaker and announced that the Foxwoode bus was leaving in ten minutes.

Luke pulled her off to a nook next to a vending machine.

"So, do you think I can see you again?" Luke shoved his hands in his pockets.

By now, she knew that Luke was seventeen and lived in Royal Oak, just twenty minutes from her house.

"Yeah, that would be fun." The words coming out of her mouth sounded stupid. Apparently, she had not said anything awkward enough to turn off Luke. They exchanged numbers. He promised to text her when they returned to the land of cell phone reception.

"The Detroit Zoo is right near my house. Maybe I can show you around sometime?" he said with his irresistible smile.

Brynlei didn't have the heart to tell him that she hated zoos. She couldn't stand seeing all of the wild animals trapped in enclosures, their eyes empty, wondering what they had done to deserve their fate. It was like torture watching the penguins swimming in circles, never reaching a destination. The monkeys were the worst. She couldn't bear to look at the monkeys staring at the walls painted like a rain forest, as if they were fooled. Brynlei felt their suffering so deeply that she believed she must have been a monkey or a penguin trapped in a zoo in one of her past lives.

"That would be fun," she said, not wanting Luke to be aware of all of her issues just yet.

Before she knew what was happening, Luke leaned in and kissed her on the cheek. It was different from the way Colton had kissed her. Luke's kiss was quick and respectable. One that said, "I had fun tonight, I like you, and there will be more kisses to follow." She smiled at Luke and walked out to the bus, her feet barely touching the ground.

* * * *

The steady summer rain tapered off by morning and was replaced with hazy sunshine and a gentle breeze streaming through the screen window. Brynlei wondered if everything that happened the night before was a dream. Then, as soon as she sat up in her bunk, Kaitlyn spoke to her from across the room.

"Brynlei, seriously? That Luke guy was so cute and nice. He was so into you. You have to let us know when you go out with him again."

They had already had this conversation on the bus ride home last night, but she didn't mind talking about Luke again. Kaitlyn seemed genuinely happy for her.

"Yeah," Brynlei said. "He seems too good to be true, but I'll let you know how it goes."

Brynlei was scared to get her hopes up. She remembered how happy she let herself feel when she thought Colton was going to be her boyfriend. How painful it was when he never called her, or talked to her, or even looked at her for that matter. How betrayed she'd felt when he lied to the rest of the school about what had happened in that room, all the stories he'd made up about how far they'd gone. Outside of the kissing part, it wasn't true. Something felt different with Luke. She'd be cautiously optimistic.

"Alyssa, did you have fun last night?" Anna smiled.

Brynlei wished Anna could just ignore Alyssa, but Anna thrived on confrontation especially when she was agitated. Alyssa's behavior at the bowling alley had provoked her. Like a dog getting poked by a stick one too many times, she had to fight back.

"Not really, Anna." Alyssa rolled her eyes. "Those guys were lame anyway. I can't wait to see Bryce again."

Anna stared down Alyssa. "The only lame person last night was you."

Thick silence hung in the cabin. No one dared to breathe. Brynlei didn't understand why Anna would call out Alyssa in front of everyone. The seconds that passed seemed like hours. Alyssa laughed sarcastically and then pursed her lips, her blue eyes latched onto Anna's black outlined eyes, neither willing to look away. Brynlei had a feeling Anna was going to pay.

"At least I don't have ugly blue hair. Freak." Alyssa zipped up her boots and stomped out of the cabin toward the mess hall.

"I'm sure she didn't mean that," McKenzie said before she followed Alyssa.

"Like I care," Anna said.

The other girls finished getting ready in silence, throwing each other shrugs and looks of disbelief. They filtered out to the mess hall. It was a lot of drama to handle before eight in the morning. Brynlei wasn't a coffee drinker, but she thought now might be a good time to start.

She and Anna hung back and waited for everyone to leave.

"You shouldn't have messed with her," Brynlei said.

"It's fun to mess with her." Anna smirked. "Anyway, I got rid of everyone, didn't I? Now we have an extra fifteen minutes to do research before anyone notices we're missing."

Was Anna's confrontation with Alyssa a coincidence or part of her master plan? Either way it worked. Anna was a good ally. They headed out as if they were going to the mess hall, but stopped when they reached the office. Brynlei peered through the screen door into an empty office. Anna slowly opened the door.

"Wait," Brynlei said. "I'll go in and do the research. You wait out here and alert me if anyone is coming."

Anna shrugged at Brynlei's sudden burst of bravery. She stepped back and let Brynlei take the lead.

"I'll say, 'I hope they're serving pancakes this morning' if I see someone coming," Anna said.

"Okay." Brynlei's heart pumped violently. She entered the office, carefully closing the door behind her. She rolled back Debbie's office chair and balanced gingerly on the edge of it. Other than riding off the trail with Anna, this was the only time Brynlei had deliberately broken a rule. They were supposed to ask permission to use the computer, but obviously that wouldn't fly for what she needed to do. The computer was in sleep mode. She pushed a key to wake it up. A box asking for a password popped up. Her heart sank. She didn't know why, but she hadn't anticipated this.

"Anna, pssst," Brynlei said in a loud whisper.

"What?"

"Do you know the password?"

"Try 'Foxwoode'. I think I remember it from last summer."

Brynlei took a deep breath and typed in "Foxwoode." Sure enough, the internet search box appeared on the screen. She made a mental note to suggest a stronger password to the Olsons after this was all over.

Her fingers trembled, as she typed in the search terms, "Caroline Watson" and "Foxwoode". Almost immediately, a list of ten articles popped up on the screen. Brynlei clicked on the first one and began reading as fast as she could.

> No Viable Persons of Interest in Case of Missing Rider
> Facing pressure from the mother and stepfather of the missing fifteen year-old girl, Caroline Watson, police brought in several possible witnesses and persons of interest for questioning. Bruce Haslow, a twenty-five year-old barn hand who began working at Foxwoode four months prior to Caroline Watson's disappearance, was the first to be questioned. The

Mission Point chief of police gave the following statement at this morning's press conference: "Mr. Haslow has been cooperating with the investigation. He was not on Foxwoode's premises at the time of Caroline Watson's disappearance. He was volunteering at the local Humane Society. Mr. Haslow's alibi was corroborated by the staff at the Humane Society and he is not considered a person of interest."

In addition to Bruce Haslow, five of Caroline Watson's cabin mates were brought in for questioning and released without suspicion. "We hope to put to rest the rumors that are circulating that these girls attacked Caroline in the woods and left her to die. We have determined these rumors are not true. By all accounts, her cabin mates are friends with Caroline and are devastated. Several witnesses reported seeing these girls swimming and laying on the beach on the afternoon of the disappearance. We have no reason to believe that any of them were involved in this incident."

The article continued...

Foxwoode's owners, Tom and Debbie Olson, have been cooperating fully with the investigation and have complied with the searches of Foxwoode's property.

Brynlei's eyes scanned to a close-up photo of Caroline's face, a school picture from the year before she disappeared. Caroline really was beautiful and exotic, with her long gleaming black hair, luminous skin, and piercing green eyes. It was easy to see how other girls could be jealous of her. No matter which designer labels they wore or how much make-up they applied, their looks would have paled in comparison to someone like Caroline. Another headline further down the screen caught her eyes. Brynlei clicked on it.

Vigil Held for Missing Girl

Family, friends, acquaintances, and community leaders gathered at Kettleman High School to pray for the recovery and safe return of Caroline Watson, the fifteen year-old girl who went missing on a trail ride at Foxwoode Riding Academy in

Mission Point, Michigan, last week. Caroline is scheduled to enter her junior year at Kettleman High this fall. She is an honor roll student and accomplished equestrian with dreams of becoming a veterinarian. "Caroline is nice to everyone she meets. She's the smartest person I've ever known," said classmate, Melody Remnar. Hundreds of people gathered, lit candles, and sang songs in an effort to let Caroline know they are not giving up. Caroline's mother and stepfather led a group prayer and thanked everyone for attending.

Brynlei's eyes swam through the words as fast as they could. She needed to get through as much as possible, afraid to come up for air. She clicked on the next article, written two days after the first one. A photo of a woman who looked like an older version of Caroline with cropped, black hair appeared on the screen. A man wearing a police uniform stood next to the woman and stared directly into the camera with sunken eyes and angular face.

Parents of Missing Lansing-Area Girl Plead for Answers
"'We just want to find Caroline. I want to bring her home and hug her," said Janet Watson, the mother of the fifteen year-old girl who has been missing for four days. Caroline's biological father, Jake Watson, was tragically killed three years ago by a stray bullet. Caroline's stepfather, Steve McDaniel, has been instrumental in recruiting volunteers to search for the girl.

Watson was last seen riding into the remote woods by herself at the Foxwoode Riding Academy in Mission Point, MI. McDaniel pleaded for additional volunteers, saying, "She could be laying somewhere out there in the woods, injured. If she is immobile, we need to find her before the elements or wild animals get to her. We won't give up." McDaniel, a twelve-year veteran of the Greater Lansing Police Force has already organized two of his own searches in the woods surrounding the Foxwoode trail system. Both searches came up empty.

The day after her disappearance, searchers found one of Caroline's riding boots floating in the Big Rapids River.

Sources close to the investigation report blood found on the outside of the boot and on a nearby rock, along with strands of Caroline's hair. Divers searched portions of the river on Monday, but no other sign of Caroline was discovered.

Police say this is an unusually difficult case due to the vastness of the forest surrounding the trails and the swift current and rocky bottom of the river. They have questioned numerous suspects, including a barn hand at Foxwoode, several of Watson's cabin mates, hikers who were seen in the area the day before the disappearance, and a known sex offender who lives less than three miles from Foxwoode Riding Academy. However, Mission Point Police have verified the whereabouts of all individuals and are no longer pursuing those leads at this time.

"The further we delve into this investigation, the more the evidence indicates that this was likely a terrible accident. We have not found any evidence of foul play so far. Caroline was not wearing a helmet when she left on the trail ride by herself. It is very possible that her saddle slid off and she hit her head on a rock and fell into the river. It is possible, though unlikely, that a bear or coyote scared her horse and attacked her when she fell off. We don't know for sure. If we don't find her before winter, we may never know. We are operating on the presumption that she is still alive, so we will keep searching."

Brynlei was amazed that Bruce and the girls in Caroline's cabin had been cleared so quickly. Someone at the Humane Society confirmed Bruce's whereabouts on that Thursday afternoon. Perhaps her recent feelings toward Bruce were wrong after all. Maybe he was just an awkward barn hand who loved animals.

It seemed like Caroline's cabin mates were never really suspects at all. Sure, the police questioned the girls, but it would have been easy for them to cover for each other. She had never thought of the other gruesome possibility: that Caroline had been eaten by a bear or torn apart by coyotes. The image made Brynlei shudder. That would explain why Caroline's body was never found. Just a boot with a few drops of blood.

Who did she see in woods? It had to have been a ghost. She kept reading. Three months later, another article appeared in *The Mission Point Herald*.

Missing Foxwoode Girl Presumed Dead
All indications point to deadly accident... Police have concluded that Caroline Watson fell off her horse, hit her head, and drowned in the Big Rapids River. All DNA found at the scene belonged to Watson. Due to the strong current, deep water levels, rocky riverbed, and extremely cold water, it's possible her body may never be recovered. "Contrary to popular belief, dead bodies don't always float," stated a forensic expert involved with the Watson investigation. "Extremely cold water temperatures often prevent bodies from surfacing, as they would in warmer temperatures. The reality of the situation is that her body may never be found."

Brynlei skimmed faster now, not wanting to miss any clues.

Foxwoode Riding Academy Settles with Parents of Missing Girl
The lawsuit filed last month in Big Rapids County Circuit Court by Janet and Steve McDaniel, the mother and stepfather of missing fifteen year-old, Caroline Watson, has resulted in an out-of-court settlement. The McDaniel's lawsuit sought $1 million in damages, alleging negligence on behalf of Foxwoode in allowing Watson to be injured, killed, or otherwise harmed one year ago...
Foxwoode's attorneys stated that their client has reached a settlement agreement with the McDaniels for an undisclosed amount in order to avoid the stress and expense of defending a lawsuit, as well as to avoid publicity that could harm their business.

As Brynlei drank in the words, she heard Anna talking outside. Brynlei snapped back into action and clicked on another article, this one farther down. It was from the Lansing Herald, written only eight months earlier.

Family Tragedy Continues: Stepfather of Missing Girl Dies in Drunk Driving Accident

Steve McDaniel, a fifteen-year veteran of the Greater Lansing Police force, drove a police cruiser into a tree at approximately 1:02 am today. He died on impact at the age of forty-five. No one else was injured in the accident. McDaniel was last seen leaving the Alley Tavern after drinking heavily. Friends say McDaniel struggled with alcoholism for years, but refused to get help. "He's always been a drinker," said James Whitehall, a close friend, "but his drinking really escalated after his step-daughter, Caroline, went missing three years ago. He couldn't deal with not knowing what happened to her."

She wanted to read more. It seemed unfair that so much tragedy could follow one family. Her heart hurt for Caroline's mom. How could one person endure so much? First, losing her husband, then her only child, and now her second husband.

"I hope they're serving pancakes for breakfast." Anna's voice was artificially loud.

Brynlei forced herself to tear her eyes from the words on the screen. She clicked on the X in the upper right corner, just as the office door swung open. Brynlei spun around in the chair, beads of sweat forming on her forehead. Debbie towered in front of her.

"Brynlei, what are you doing?"

Brynlei was surprised that Debbie knew her name, but she guessed that was her job.

"I just wanted to check my email. I'm sorry. I know I should have asked first." Brynlei wished she could crawl beneath the desk.

"Yes, you should have," Debbie said. "But go ahead."

"Oh, I did it already. Thanks." Brynlei jumped up. She couldn't get out of the chair fast enough. Debbie's mouth curled into an odd half-smile, as if she knew an inside joke and Brynlei did not.

"You girls are going to be the end of me. Go get some breakfast before the mess hall closes."

Right," Brynlei said, as she rushed out the door. She took a deep breath of fresh air, grateful for her narrow escape. She could only hope Debbie didn't go back and check the search history. Brynlei hadn't had time to delete it. Anna stood next to a tree a few feet away. Her eyes were wide with questions.

"Did she see?"

"No. I don't think so. But I don't think she believed me either." Brynlei kept her head low.

They walked up the hill to the mess hall. In a quiet voice, Brynlei recounted everything she had found on the computer, and Anna listened intently. Although the articles shed some light on the specifics of Caroline's disappearance, Brynlei and Anna realized they now had even more questions than before. They hadn't known about the sex offender who lived nearby or the hikers who were seen the day before. Of course, they had all been cleared, just like Bruce and the other five girls in Caroline's cabin. Yet how had the police cleared them so quickly?

"Maybe Alyssa was right," Anna said. "Maybe the police are stupid."

Brynlei had to admit, the same thought had crossed her mind.

Chapter Twelve

The atmosphere during the morning lesson was even more serious than usual. The Foxwoode horse show was approaching in less than a week and every one of the Flying Foxes wanted to win a blue ribbon in front of her family and friends. Every one of them believed, at least in the back of their minds, that they had a shot at winning the Top Rider award. Realistically, the Top Rider competition was between Alyssa and Anna at this point, but Brynlei would still aim for an upset.

On top of the pressure of the impending show, there was the palpable hatred between Alyssa and Anna. Anna seemed to be channeling her anger productively toward her riding. She looked like perfection as she cut diagonally across the ring and asked Rebel for a flying lead change. They all strove to appear effortless on top of their horses, but Anna pulled it off better than anyone. Her shoulders stayed back, her eyes looked ahead, her heels pushed down, her elbows bent, her hands maintaining a light contact with the bit, and her legs stuck to Rebel's side at precisely the correct angle. Alyssa looked effortless, too, but Bentley was a highly-trained horse that could probably make anyone look good. Brynlei knew from experience that Rebel was not an easy ride.

Brynlei held Jett to a collected canter and prepared to cut across the ring to ask him for a flying lead change. Jett bounced a little in the middle and swapped leads. Now they were cantering in the opposite direction, following the other horses.

"Remember to change your bend when you ask for the lead change," Miss Jill said after Brynlei had crossed.

It was usually easy for Brynlei to focus on her riding, especially during her lessons. Riding was an escape from the constant thoughts that fluttered through her mind. When she concentrated on maintaining her position, channeling her horse's energy, counting her strides, and remembering her courses, there was no room for anything else. She had to be in the moment. Today was different. The surroundings distracted her. She knew to change her bend after the lead change, but she forgot to apply pressure to her inside leg because she was looking at Debbie out of the corner of her eye. Debbie sat on the bleachers at the edge of the ring with a clipboard in her lap, watching the girls. Every once in a while, she jotted something on her pad of paper. Everyone knew Debbie influenced who would receive the Top Rider award. She was obviously judging them.

Miss Jill called the girls to the center of the ring and instructed them to jump the two diagonal fences until she told them to stop. Kaitlyn and Alyssa went first, following each other over the fences in a figure-eight pattern. They both rode well and found their distances easily, but then Daisey's pace slowed, her canter dull. Daisey chipped in before the jumps twice in a row.

"Maintain a constant pace," Miss Jill yelled, placing her hands on her hips. "Do two more."

Hopefully, Alyssa would chip in, too, or worse. But Alyssa and Bentley flew flawlessly over the jumps, finding the perfect distance each time. They performed for their audience.

Anna and McKenzie were up next. Brynlei held her breath for Anna. Anna would need to ride the fences perfectly to measure up to Alyssa. As Anna rode around the corner of the ring, something in the woods caught Brynlei's eye. The fine hairs on her neck and arms bristled.

She sensed someone or something watching her in the background. She thought she saw a flash of movement in the trees beyond. It was there and then it was gone. Just a shadow, perhaps. Maybe an animal. Yet it had to be more than that. She'd felt this energy before—the last time she spotted the girl with the long dark hair in the woods. Or was it Bruce hiding there?

Her eyes no longer followed Anna over the fences. They were fixed on the dense trees behind the ring. A branch snapped in the distance, but she couldn't make out anything through the trees. A stiff breeze brushed by her cheeks and rustled the leaves, preventing her from hearing anything else.

"Excellent, Anna," Miss Jill said, jolting Brynlei back to the lesson. "Nice job making Rebel wait."

Brynlei had missed Anna's jumps, but she gathered Anna was giving Alyssa a run for her money.

"Brynlei and Julia, you can go," Miss Jill said.

Brynlei's thoughts were still on the stirring in the woods, but she took a deep breath, sat back, and asked Jett to canter. Jett's canter felt off-balance and she immediately realized Jett had picked up the wrong lead. She stopped him, organized her reins, and asked him to canter again. This time, they picked up the correct lead, but Brynlei had already lost points with Debbie, who looked on from the bleachers, expressionless, and writing occasionally on her clipboard. Now Brynlei and Jett followed five strides behind Julia and Devon toward the first jump. She tried to concentrate on the jump, on her position, on her strides. One, two, three. She counted her strides up to the jump and found a good distance. Maybe there was a chance she could recover from her rough start, if she could just stay focused.

As she rounded the far corner near the woods and approached the next jump, something moved again in her peripheral vision. Her eyes were pulled toward the trees like a magnet to metal. There, for a split second, two emerald eyes stared at her from behind the dense forest wall. The orbs glowed against the pale white face that held them. Brynlei's gaze locked onto the green eyes a moment before they disappeared.

By the time Brynlei looked up, the next jump was directly in front of her. Without any guidance from his rider, Jett veered off to the left. Brynlei hung in the air, and then landed with a thud on the ground. The sandy footing in the ring cushioned her landing, but she was humiliated. The air hissed out of Brynlei like a popped party balloon. She'd fallen off right in front of Debbie. Any slim chance she might have had at winning Top Rider was now officially gone.

Miss Jill held Jett's reins in one hand and helped Brynlei to her feet with the other hand. Debbie had abandoned her post on the bleachers and was now leaning over the fence, her forehead crinkled in concern.

"Are you okay, Brynlei," Debbie asked.

"Yes." Brynlei avoided eye contact with everyone as she brushed the dirt from her breeches.

Without a word, Miss Jill gave Brynlei a leg up and instructed her to start over. Brynlei was determined to save face. She organized her reins, picked up a canter, and rode the next six jumps in a row to near perfection.

"Good recovery, Brynlei." Miss Jill winked at her. She must have felt Brynlei's disappointment.

The lesson continued for another forty-five minutes, as Debbie looked on. Every once in a while, a gust of wind caught a section of Debbie's sculpted hair and held it hostage in the air before letting it down. Brynlei ordered herself to pay attention to her riding. Stop looking at Debbie. Don't look at the woods, she reminded herself until her eyes obeyed. She would investigate the woods as soon as the lesson was over.

Somehow, she made it through without getting distracted again, although her performance was far from perfect. At least Anna had ridden impressively throughout. She wished Anna would win Top Rider. She deserved it more than anyone.

As soon as the lesson ended, Brynlei cooled off Jett as quickly as possible and turned him out in his spacious paddock. She didn't want to waste any time talking to anyone, not even Anna. She jogged away from the barn, darting behind the tree line toward the spot where she saw the green eyes watching her. When she arrived at the precise area, she was not surprised to find it empty. Her boot stuck in the mud as she tried to take another step.

She looked down and saw footprints in the mud. Only slightly larger than her own size seven feet. There were several prints overlapping, then turning and heading off into the woods. Brynlei began to follow, but the tracks soon disappeared as the bed of pine needles on the forest floor became thicker. She struggled to suck in air as she turned and ran back toward Cabin 5. Some of the pieces of the puzzle were starting to come together—the long black hair, the green eyes, and now the footprints. She needed to tell Anna what she had just discovered. It wasn't a ghost. Caroline Watson was alive and living in these woods.

Brynlei walked back to the barn as fast as she could. She attempted to appear casual. She didn't want to arouse suspicion. Rebel was already in his paddock and Anna was gone. Brynlei made a beeline for Cabin 5, where she found Anna washing her face in the bathroom.

"Hang back before lunch," Brynlei whispered into Anna's ear. She placed a finger to her lips, signaling not to say another word. It was too risky.

They waited for the other girls to leave for the mess hall, watching from the window until they were well out of earshot. Then the words flooded from Brynlei. She told Anna why she fell off during the lesson and about the pale face from behind the trees, the haunting green eyes, and the footprints in the mud.

"It had to be Caroline." Brynlei heard the frantic edge to her voice.

"Yeah," Anna said, staring wide-eyed at Brynlei. "That's crazy. Why didn't anyone else see her?"

"Sometimes I sense things that other people miss! I told you that already!" Brynlei yelled in frustration at being so close to discovering something and not being able to figure it out.

"Okay. You don't need to get mad. I'm on your side, remember?" Anna threw her hands up in the air.

"Sorry." Brynlei rarely lost control of her outward emotions and embarrassment took over. She stared at the uneven planks that made up the bathroom floor. The floorboards squeaked beneath her feet like angry mice.

"Show me the footprints and then let's go eat lunch." Anna was already halfway out the door before Brynlei caught up to her.

They ran toward the woods behind Ring A, looking over their shoulders every few seconds to make sure no one was watching them. They had to hurry before people started noticing they weren't at lunch. When they approached the spot where she'd found the footprints, Brynlei's stomach dropped.

"They were right here." Her mouth was dry and she could barely speak. Leaves and twigs covered the ground where the footprints had been. She frantically brushed them away. The mud was smeared underneath, as if someone had run their foot back and forth over the prints. "Someone tried to cover it up."

Anna studied the smeared mud under the leaves. The color drained from her already pale face as she stepped out from the cover of the woods and looked around at the empty grounds.

"Dude." Anna made her way back to Brynlei. "I'm freaked out right now."

Brynlei didn't say anything, but she was scared, too. She'd had the feeling of being watched, or followed, almost from the moment she arrived at Foxwoode. Now she had proof that her feelings were legitimate. The girls crept toward the mess hall, certain that someone, somewhere was watching them. Brynlei focused on each step she took, as if a landmine might explode under her at any point. They needed to figure out what to do next.

They sat alone at a table in the corner of the large wooden room, nibbling their hummus and cucumber wraps in silence.

Finally, Brynlei spoke under her breath. "She's real. We need to find her."

"Someone doesn't want us to," Anna whispered. "Maybe we should call the police."

"Sure, and tell them what? That we saw the ghost of a girl who might be real and then we saw footprints that aren't there anymore?"

"I don't know." Anna ran her fingers through her hair. "I'm sure if there is a chance that we saw Caroline Watson, the police would want to check it out."

"They won't believe us." Brynlei looked around to make sure no one was listening to their conversation. "We need to go into the woods again and look for her."

"When? It's hard to do anything around here without people watching."

"We can sneak out at night," Brynlei said. "When everyone is asleep. We have flashlights."

"Are you crazy?" Anna raised her eyebrows. "Take the horses out at night?"

"Horses can see in the dark. Or we could go on foot." Brynlei struggled to keep her voice even. She wanted Anna to know she was doing this.

Anna ate her sandwich and stared out the window without saying anything.

"Don't you want to know who's out there and why?" Brynlei asked.

"Yes." There was a tone of determination in Anna's voice that Brynlei was happy to hear. "But we need time to make a plan first. Let's go tomorrow night."

* * * *

Brynlei and Anna were the last ones to leave the mess hall. They walked back to Cabin 5 without speaking, each of them deep in thought. Brynlei was thankful Anna was at Foxwoode with her. She couldn't imagine trying to figure this all out on her own. She wondered if she and Anna ever would have become friends anywhere else under different circumstances. Probably not. She would have been scared to approach someone like Anna, with her blue hair and nose ring, if she hadn't been forced to speak to her bunk mate that first day in their cabin.

The sugary-sour scent of watermelon, blue raspberry, and sour apple candy wafted in the wind. Up ahead, Alyssa, McKenzie, Kaitlyn, and Julia filed out of the store, carrying bags of gummy bears and licorice. They had a routine of stocking up on candy before heading to the beach. Brynlei and Anna met up with the group and walked with them toward Cabin 5.

"Hi ladies," Julia said. "Want a sour worm?"

Brynlei took a sour worm out of Julia's hand, not wanting to be rude. She was about to take her second bite out of the stretchy candy when they reached the cabin. As Kaitlyn pulled open the door, the conversation halted abruptly. Everyone stopped and stared, mouths hanging open in shock. A ragged, pink teddy bear dangled in mid-air from Anna's top bunk, a rope wrapped around its neck. Someone had plucked its eyes out and bits of white stuffing oozed from holes where the eyes had been. A torn piece of paper was pinned to the bear's stomach. As the bear swung slowly back and forth, Brynlei could barely make out the words scrawled in pencil on the paper. *Leave Freak.*

Brynlei turned and looked at Anna. The flash of fear in Anna's eyes quickly turned to fury as she turned on Alyssa.

"You think that's funny?"

"Kind of." Alyssa appeared completely unfazed by the dangling bear. "Hey, it wasn't me."

"Yeah, right."

For a second, Brynlei thought Anna was going to punch Alyssa in her perfect little face. Instead, Anna lunged toward her disfigured bear and began untying the rope. Her fingers pulled frantically at the knot around the bear's neck. Tears streamed down Anna's face. Brynlei didn't know what to say, so she reached over and put her hand on Anna's back. She could feel Anna's heart pounding violently beneath her smoldering flesh.

"Oh, tough girl isn't so tough after all." Alyssa couldn't contain her laughter as she continued popping licorice bites into her mouth.

McKenzie stood next to Alyssa, but didn't laugh for once.

"That's so not cool, Alyssa," Kaitlyn said. She took a step back from Alyssa, as if trying to distance herself.

"You crossed the line, Alyssa. You should apologize." Julia set her candy down and started picking up loose pieces of stuffing off the floor.

"I didn't do anything." Alyssa threw her hands in the air.

"I'm not going to leave." Although tears no longer leaked from Anna's eyes, drips of black mascara now streaked her cheeks giving her the appearance of a disheveled warrior. "I'm not leaving until I win Top Rider, you spoiled piece of crap!"

"Whatever, Anna." Alyssa rolled her eyes. "I'm sorry about your bear, but it wasn't me." Apparently, Alyssa recognized the other girls were turning on her because she spent the next several minutes denying any involvement in the hanging of the bear and trying to pass out her remaining candy to the others.

"I couldn't have done it," Alyssa persisted. "I was at lunch with you guys, remember?"

No one really believed her, though. No one, that is, except Brynlei.

Chapter Thirteen

During free time, Brynlei and Anna stuck together, despite Kaitlyn's pleas for them to join the others on a trail ride.

"Thanks, but I'm going to take a nap on the beach," Anna said. "It's been a long day."

"Me, too." Brynlei stared at the floor, worried her face would give her away.

"Okay, then we'll see you at dinner," Kaitlyn said as she bounced out the door.

Brynlei admired Kaitlyn's efforts to ensure Anna felt welcome as part of the group. She could imagine Kaitlyn leading the anti-bullying rallies at her high school, encouraging everyone to wear orange, asking the awkward girl to sit with her at lunch, and condemning those who ridiculed the different ones. Kaitlyn was upbeat and inclusive in a way that wasn't forced or manufactured. People couldn't help but like her.

Brynlei and Anna left the other girls in the cabin and headed to the beach in silence. They found their usual spot a few feet away from the lapping water of Lake Foxwoode. The beach was relatively empty as dark clouds drifted closer. They spread out their towels and sat down. Only three younger girls sat in a group in the distance, talking in quiet voices to each other. The clouds hung unusually low in the sky, as if trying to listen in on their conversation. Brynlei wondered what secrets those other girls were keeping.

"Are you okay?" Brynlei asked, after she'd given up trying to hear what the girls were saying.

"Yeah," Anna said. "Alyssa is a horrible person. I'm not going to let her get to me."

"I agree." Brynlei paused and looked around. "I don't think she's the one who hung your bear."

"What?" Anna's eyes almost bulged out of her head. "You believe her?"

"It's more like, I think whoever covered up the footprints is trying to scare us," Brynlei said.

"Caroline?" Anna suggested. "Or Bruce? Or the Olsons? Or some random kidnapper? You think they broke into our cabin and mutilated my bear?"

"I don't know. It could have been any of them, or someone else. That's what we need to find out."

Anna and Brynlei gazed out at the dark, murky waters of Lake Foxwoode.

"We must be close to figuring this thing out. Whoever is trying to stop us wouldn't have risked going into our cabin and getting caught," Anna said.

"So you agree with me?"

"Yes. I guess you're right. It wasn't Alyssa. She isn't smart enough to pull that off."

"Ha." Brynlei smiled in agreement.

"I'm still going to win Top Rider, though. Just so she doesn't get it." Anna dug her heels into the sand.

"I have no doubt about that," Brynlei said, her eyes still fixated on the rippling, black water of the lake.

"Now we need a plan."

They spent the next hour and a half outlining everything they knew about Caroline's disappearance. They talked in hushed voices and recorded their insights in a red spiral notebook Brynlei carried in her beach bag.

Brynlei constantly scanned the tree line across the lake for any movement. She looked over her shoulder every thirty seconds to see if anyone was watching them. Since finding the footprints, they were almost positive Caroline was alive and living somewhere in the woods. Brynlei wrote down everything she could remember from the articles she'd found online. She and Anna made a list of all the times and locations where Brynlei had seen Caroline, starting with the first day

118

when her parents took the wrong turn down the service drive. Brynlei now believed the figure she'd glimpsed next to the tool shed was Caroline.

They wrote down any landmarks that would help them find their way through the woods at night—the Blue Trail, the wild raspberry bushes, the creek. Brynlei drew a crude map on top of the Foxwoode trail map. She created icons that represented various landmarks and the locations of the sightings. The map reminded her of the pirate maps she and Derek used to make when they were kids. The only thing lacking was a giant red X where the treasure was buried. Rather than an X, she drew a red circle around the area where they believed they were most likely to find Caroline, or at least some kind of clue relating to her disappearance.

The target area was deep in the woods beyond the spot where Brynlei had spotted Caroline helping Rebel. It was farther than they'd ever gone into the woods before. Brynlei studied the map they'd created, admiring their targeted approach, burning it into her memory.

Almost everyone at Foxwoode was in bed by ten, but they needed to wait until after the midnight bunk check before leaving the cabin. Anna suggested drinking coffee before bed to ensure they didn't fall asleep, too, but Brynlei thought that would raise too many questions from the cabin mates. She didn't like the taste of coffee. They agreed to pour diet Coke into their water bottles instead.

They would wear black and leave the cabin in darkness, with flashlights turned off, until they reached the cover of the Blue Trail. They would travel the trail on foot, running or jogging to cover ground faster. They decided the horses would be too much of a liability at night. They'd need to cut through the thick brush off the trail and travel through narrow gaps deep into the woods. The horses might not fit.

They would follow a line Brynlei drew on the map in the approximate place where they had seen Caroline run into the woods after she untangled Rebel from his reins. From there, they'd make their way toward the red circle on the map and search for evidence. Anna had a compass attached to her key chain that she would use to guide them through the woods and, hopefully, to find their way back again. They would need to be back in their bunks by four or four thirty at the latest.

The barn hands and kitchen staff woke up early.

Their plan had one major weakness. They weren't exactly sure what they were looking for, aside from Caroline herself. Even then, they didn't know what they would do if they found her. Hold her captive? Demand answers? They couldn't think that far ahead yet. They had to start somewhere and they would know a clue when they saw it.

Brynlei could sense if something was amiss or if someone was nearby. If they saw a stranger lurking in the woods or found an abandoned cabin, they could report it to the police. They agreed to wait until after the horse show to report anything, though. They were breaking the rules and neither of them wanted to get kicked out of Foxwoode.

* * * *

The hazy sun sunk lower in the sky. It was almost five o'clock. They shook the sand out of their towels and Brynlei slid the red notebook deep into her bag. They began to trudge through the sandy trail back toward the cabins. As they rounded the bend in the path, a shiver ran through her, like an unwelcome jolt of electricity. She stopped abruptly and Anna bumped into her back.

"What's wrong? Is your Spidey-sense tingling?" Anna said.

Brynlei looked up. Bruce leaned against a nearby tree, a saw dangling from his hand. A few stray branches lay in a pile of sawdust on the ground. Bruce's eyes drilled into Brynlei first, then Anna. His icy stare immobilized them.

How long had he been there? Had he been watching them the whole time? Brynlei's mind was in a panic. Her body told her to run, but somehow she managed to stand motionless next to Anna. Before things became too awkward, Bruce nodded at them and averted his eyes toward the overgrown tree. He began sawing steadily at a jagged branch that encroached upon the path to the beach. The girls trained their eyes on the ground as they darted around Bruce and headed for the safety of their cabin.

An hour later, Brynlei sat across from Anna at a long rectangular table in the mess hall. Kaitlyn sidled up next to Anna and Julia sat next to Brynlei. Alyssa and McKenzie sat across from each other at the other end of the table. It was spaghetti night again and the pungent smell of onions, tomatoes, ground beef, olive oil, and garlic permeated the air.

"Anna, I don't want to bring up a bad topic or anything," Kaitlyn said, "but I know how to sew. I can fix the eyes on your bear. Seriously, I mean it. I have my sewing kit with me."

"Thanks, but don't worry about it. My mom can sew him when I get back home." Anna's face revealed no expression, as she twirled her spaghetti around her fork.

Brynlei tried to imagine anyone related to Anna being able to sew. She couldn't form the image in her mind. She suspected Anna really just wanted everyone to forget the fact that she slept with a pink teddy bear.

"Okay, but let me know if you change your mind. I love sewing." As she said the words, Kaitlyn smiled warmly and squeezed Anna's arm, making an effort to let Anna know she was her friend in case there was any doubt before.

The dinner continued with Kaitlyn describing a dress she had sewn for her baby cousin the previous fall. After she had completed all the measuring, the cutting, the sewing, the dress was three sizes too small.

"I decided it would be perfect for my cousin's baby doll instead." Kaitlyn threw her head back and laughed, like it was the funniest story anyone had ever told.

Julia turned the conversation to their trail ride from earlier in the afternoon. Apparently, the girls had seen all sorts of animals, including a skunk that scampered across the trail twenty feet in front of them. Julia described how they all had frozen in fear, terrified of being sprayed. In the end, the skunk didn't even seem to notice they were there. Then they debated why a skunk would be running around during the day in the first place.

Fresh fears about their plans for the following night began to invade Brynlei's head. She hadn't thought about all the wild animals that emerge in the darkness of night. There were skunks and possums, not to mention coyotes and bears. She and Anna would have to be on the lookout for all kinds of danger.

Julia complained about how long it had taken them to stop and pick wild raspberries. Brynlei and Anna's eyes immediately found each other. To them, the wild raspberries meant one thing—a marker for where they would veer off the trail tomorrow night. They quickly looked away from

121

each other, afraid of giving away the secret they shared.

* * * *

After dinner, the cabin mates headed out for an impromptu bonfire by the lake. Brynlei locked eyes with Anna, silently asking her to stay behind. They needed to go over their plan again.

"I'm gonna stay back and just chill for a while," Anna said to the other girls. "I'll catch up with you later." No one questioned her.

"Yeah, me, too." Brynlei plopped down on her bunk and pretended to read a book.

"Okay, see you guys later!" Kaitlyn bounded out of the cabin behind Alyssa, Julia, and McKenzie.

When they were safely alone in the cabin, Brynlei spoke. "I need to brush my teeth. Then let's go over the map again." Brynlei walked to the bathroom, anxious to neutralize the layer of garlic butter that clung to her mouth.

Standing in the bathroom, Brynlei recognized the familiar creaking sound coming from the planks beneath her feet. She studied the creaky boards as she brushed her teeth, shifting her weight from foot to foot to make them squeak. Not all the planks creaked. The two planks that moaned the loudest were near the side wall. Those boards were a slightly lighter shade of honey pine than the surrounding planks. The difference was barely perceptible, yet it was there. How had she not observed this before?

Brynlei remembered the bathroom light turning on and off by itself in the middle of the night. An identical creaking sound had shot waves of panic through her then. When she thought Bruce was in the cabin, she'd also heard the same creaking sound. She'd thought it had come from the hallway, but maybe it had been from the bathroom.

Brynlei spit her toothpaste into the sink. "Anna. Come here." Anna appeared in the bathroom door a second later. "Help me with these floor boards."

Brynlei pushed and prodded the creaking planks until she found a narrow, almost invisible, gap between the boards. She ran her finger along the crack and then she felt something. A tiny string brushed her finger and sent chills throughout her body. Brynlei grasped the clear thread, which felt like dental floss, and pulled. Sure enough, the two wide planks rose up from the floor, exposing a foot or two of open air beneath the cabin before reaching the dirt ground below.

"What the—" Anna leaned over the opening, her mouth hanging open.

Brynlei could not speak. They'd just discovered a secret door in the floor of their bathroom, like something out of a haunted house or a horror movie. She wasn't crazy. Bruce had been in their cabin that day when the other girls were at the beach. It was probably him in the middle of the night, too. Or could it have been Caroline? But why?

"A trap door," Anna said, barely whispering.

She sat on the edge of the opening and lowered herself down, pulling the floor closed on top of her. Anna disappeared from the room, just like that. A moment later, the door popped open and Anna pulled herself back up into the bathroom. "Bruce is even creepier than I thought." Anna's voice shook slightly. She wasn't kidding. "We should nail it shut."

"With what?" Brynlei asked. "We don't have any tools. Besides, I don't think we should draw attention to the fact we found it. Let's stay under the radar until after we search the woods."

"Yeah, I guess you're right. No need to add fuel to the fire." Anna closed the hatch and stood on top of it, leaving nothing but a plain wood floor beneath her feet.

* * * *

Surprisingly, Brynlei slept soundly, as if her body had convinced her mind of the urgency of stockpiling her sleep before the following night. The morning crept by in slow motion, Brynlei painfully aware of the ticking of each passing second. As time marched slowly forward, a nervous energy consumed her body. She struggled to quell the mismatched combination of dread and excitement that bubbled beneath the surface. Like trying to shake together oil and vinegar, the two competing emotions didn't mix well. She felt high as a kite one moment, almost giddy with the thought of discovering the secret of Caroline Watson, only to crash into a wall of fear the next moment. A fear so real it left her struggling to breathe. Having Anna on her side was her strength. Anna acted calm, cool, and collected, as usual. They were going to do this together. Brynlei was the one who had dragged Anna into this in the first place. She couldn't turn back.

The morning riding lesson seemed to stretch on for hours. Brynlei tried to appear unruffled, like Anna. She forced herself to focus on her riding and used her special breathing techniques. While she might have fooled the others in the ring, Jett was not convinced. He must have sensed the conflict between Brynlei's outward demeanor and her inner turmoil. He became increasingly nervous and agitated. Brynlei could barely hold it all together.

Then it was lunchtime. Brynlei found herself in the mess hall, choking down a black bean and chickpea salad. She couldn't remember walking to the mess hall or choosing her food or finding a table, although she must have because she was there sitting next to Anna. Her mind wandered down a faraway path of woods, darkness, and secrets.

Then she was back inside Cabin 5. Anna and the others went to their bunks, but Brynlei entered the bathroom. She needed a moment alone, just to breathe. She shivered when she saw the secret floor planks near the wall, which appeared just as she and Anna had left them. Washing her face and reapplying her sunscreen would make her feel better. She reached up to the shelf and dug through her kit in search of her soap, but her fingers touched on something unfamiliar instead. Something hard, smooth, and cold. She pulled the object out of her bag. A glass bottle. She stared in confusion at the foreign object in her hand. A single serving bottle of chardonnay. The kind Brynlei had never consumed herself, but had seen her mother buy from the bin at the grocery store before attending summer concerts in the park. The seal on the bottle's cap was broken and almost all of the wine inside was gone, presumably enjoyed by someone. Brynlei immediately rushed to get the bottle out of her hand, as if the glass was burning her skin. She knew she was not supposed to have alcohol, that it could send her home, that someone had placed it there to hurt her. She lunged toward the wastebasket and threw in the bottle, burying it under bits of paper towels and tissues. She had no sooner discarded the bottle, than Miss Jill and Miss Ashley barged through the door to Cabin 5 and instructed everyone not to move.

"I'm sorry girls," Miss Jill said, "but we've received information that some of you are hiding alcohol in the cabin. We just need to do a quick search to make sure this isn't true."

Brynlei gasped for air, her mind still catching up to what was happening. She stood frozen in the doorway and watched as Miss Jill and Miss Ashley sifted through duffel bags and suitcases. The girls stared at each other in disbelief.

"Who told you that?" Anna asked, incredulous.

"We can't say," Miss Jill said. Her even tone gave nothing away.

Nobody except Brynlei seemed nervous while Miss Jill and Miss Ashley continued digging through dirty laundry and looking under beds. Hopefully, the bottle of wine was the only evidence that had been planted. Even if they discovered the bottle in the trash, it couldn't be linked to anyone in particular. Miss Jill began pulling back sheets and shaking out pillows. She came to Anna's bed and grabbed Anna's pillow. A small plastic bottle flew out of the pillowcase and slid across the floor. Bright red letters across the bottle screamed "Smirnoff Vodka".

Brynlei felt as if she was falling off a tall building. Her eyes found Anna, who now braced herself against the wall. Miss Jill lowered her gaze to the floor and shook her head, clearly disappointed.

"That's not mine," Anna protested. "Someone put it there."

"Don't even try to blame me again," Alyssa said. "I didn't do it."

"It's not hers!" Brynlei yelled. "I know it isn't!" She couldn't control the words that blurted from her mouth.

"How do you suppose a bottle of vodka came to be hidden in your pillowcase, Anna?" Miss Jill said.

"Someone doesn't want me here. That person planted it in my pillowcase." Beads of sweat gathered on Anna's forehead.

"We have different information from a very reliable person," Miss Jill said. "I'm afraid you know what this means, Anna. You've already received one warning."

"It's not mine." Anna crossed her arms and her normally pale face turned an angry shade of red.

"Rules are rules, Anna." Miss Jill sounded like a parent who had placed all her trust and hopes and dreams into her teenage daughter only to discover the daughter had been lying about their shared aspirations the whole time.

"I'll help you pack your bags and I'll have the Olsons call your parents," Miss Jill continued.

Tears pushed their way out from behind Brynlei's eyes. She could tell Miss Jill about the bottle of wine in her bathroom kit, but Brynlei didn't want to implicate herself, too. She couldn't get sent home when she was so close to discovering the secret. The vodka wasn't Anna's. Brynlei knew that, but she couldn't think of any way to prove it. Even disclosing the hidden door in the bathroom floor wouldn't prove anything. Her eyes locked with Anna's as Miss Jill led Anna out of the cabin.

"Wait," Brynlei said. "I think I know—"

"No, Brynlei." Anna interrupted her.

Anna's wide eyes pleaded with Brynlei, telling her not speak another word about any of it. Brynlei bit her tongue and nodded at Anna. As Anna walked past Brynlei, she said, "Stick with the plan," under her breath. Anna placed something in Brynlei's hand. It was her key chain compass.

Now more than ever, Brynlei had to discover the truth. Her only real friend at Foxwoode had just been ambushed. Anna, who Brynlei trusted with her life, whose treasured stuffed bear had been disfigured and hanged, who was a sure thing to win Top Rider, was being led away like a prisoner in handcuffs. It was all getting too personal.

Miss Ashley finished searching the rest of the bunks and moved to the bathroom. Brynlei's bones turned to icicles and her hands began to shake. Would Miss Ashley discover the bottle of wine in the wastebasket? Brynlei was the last person in the bathroom. The bottle had been in her kit. Surely, they would find a way to link the bottle to her.

Brynlei could not breathe, as she listened to Miss Ashley unzipping kits and rummaging through personal belongings in the bathroom. Finally, she emerged with empty hands. "All clear in the bathroom." Miss Ashley hadn't found the bottle. Brynlei drew in a long breath and exhaled.

As Brynlei staggered back toward her bunk, she noticed her beach bag askew on the floor. Even before she opened the bag, she knew. Her stomach filled with dread as her quivering hands pushed aside her beach towel and dug inside the bag. The red spiral notebook was gone.

* * * *

It took Brynlei a few hours to overcome the initial shock of being set up, of her notebook being stolen, and of Anna being unfairly sent home. When the shock subsided, flames of anger ignited and spread within her. Her blood became gasoline, pumping the burning fire throughout her body. Whoever was trying to prevent her from digging into the secret in the woods was having the opposite effect. She was more determined than ever to find Caroline Watson.

Brynlei lay in her bunk, waiting for her remaining cabin mates to succumb to sleep. She lay still and patient, as the moment of action slowly drew closer. The familiar wooden slats above her that used to hold Anna now resembled a skeleton supporting nothing but a bare mattress. Anna's parents had arrived to pick her up an hour before lights out. They didn't look anything like Brynlei had imagined. Anna's mom was a petite blonde with a pixie cut, wearing Bermuda shorts and a pink T-shirt. Brynlei would never have believed that the tiny, demure woman was Anna's mom, except for a small tattoo of a rose with spiked thorns on the woman's ankle. Her dad was a large, muscular man with thinning gray hair and kind eyes. Anna's parents' faces had swirled with confusion, disappointment, and happiness at seeing their daughter after almost three weeks. They exchanged hugs interspersed with looks of defeat, but spoke few words as they moved their daughter's belongings from the cabin into the trunk of their Lexus.

After being hung out to dry by Chrysler, Anna's dad's foreign car was apparently his own method of giving a giant middle finger to the world. Brynlei had pulled Anna into an awkward hug before Anna climbed into the backseat. She'd desperately wanted to tell Anna's parents that it was a mistake. That someone else put the vodka in Anna's pillowcase. That Anna was going to win Top Rider.

Instead, Brynlei had spit out a weak, "Bye." Then she added, "I'm going to find out who did this."

Anna had only nodded as if to say, "I know you will," and closed the car door. She gave Brynlei a sad smile as the car drove off into the night, leaving tire tracks in the soft ground behind it. Brynlei watched from the steps of the cabin as brake lights glowed red in front of the barn. Anna got out and slipped inside the barn door closest to Rebel's stall. Minutes later, Anna reemerged, her tears glistening in the headlights of the Lexus.

Brynlei lay perfectly still in her bed, fueled with vengeance after the wrong done to Anna. She was wide-awake when Miss Jill popped her head into the cabin for the midnight bunk check.

She strained to hear the breathing patterns of the other girls over the incessant chirping of the crickets outside. Her clock cast a dim green light onto her pillow. It was one thirty-five. The jagged gasping, tossing, and turning around her had eventually given way to soft, even breathing. Everyone was finally sound asleep.

After gently pulling her bag of supplies out from under the bed, Brynlei walked gingerly across the floor. She eased open the cabin door in super-slow motion and closed it carefully behind her, breathing a fleeting sigh of relief once she'd made it outside. She pulled her black shirt and black leggings out of the bag and stretched them over her pajama shorts and tank top. She tied her tennis shoes tightly to her feet, gripped the flashlight in her hand, and hid the bag under the cabin steps.

She surveyed her dark surroundings. All of the cabin lights were off, but the stars above shone down on her, threatening to give her away. She ran toward the woods.

Chapter Fourteen

The entrance to the Blue Trail emerged from the blackness about five minutes later. The woods appeared impossibly dark and dense, as if Brynlei were running into the center of the earth. Even the gleaming stars in the sky could not penetrate the darkness of the forest. Not until she was surrounded by the blackness of the trees did Brynlei dare to turn on her flashlight. The narrow circle of light that glowed from the flashlight was so weak and insufficient in comparison to the massive dark that encompassed her that she laughed at the ridiculousness of it. How many cruel jokes could be played on her in one day?

Other than illuminating the next step she was about to take, the flashlight was useless. Brynlei aimed the light at the ground in front of her so she could see any rocks or sticks that might be in her path. She continued running along the Blue Trail, powered by adrenaline and fear. Or was it revenge?

She could not shake the feeling that she was being watched, even now. Eyes could be lurking anywhere behind the curtain of darkness surrounding her. She was hyper-aware of her body, each step that she took, each breath that she inhaled and exhaled, each beat of her heart, and the prickling of ten thousand needles across her skin. Every twig that cracked under her feet caused her to bound higher in the air and run faster. Every branch that brushed her arm transformed into a hand reaching out to grab her, to stop her. Brynlei ran faster.

At last, she reached the bend in the trail that ran along the stream. She continued running until she spotted the clumps of wild raspberry bushes sprouting from the darkness. They looked different at night, more like the wretched, knotty hands of a hundred witches clawing at her than the inviting berry plants of the daylight. The bushes were her signal to turn off the trail and head due north.

Although she no longer had her map, she remembered in detail the path she had planned to follow. She pushed her way through the raspberry bushes, cutting her hand on the thorns before emerging on the other side. The thick brush off the trail forced her to slow her pace. She pulled out the key chain compass Anna had slipped to her and followed the N symbol. She would need to continue north for another half-mile to arrive near the spot where she'd seen Caroline holding Rebel by the reins.

Brynlei slowed to a jog. The wayward sticks and branches swiping at her ankles and face were slowing her down. Then a branch snapped far off to her right. She stopped and listened. A rustling noise echoed in the distance. She held her breath. The crackling of leaves and branches was getting closer.

Whatever was making the noise was an animal, not a person. The steps were light and uneven, and the rustling sound scampered this way and that through the trees. She shone the weak ray of light in the direction of the noise, hoping to spot something. She prayed to catch a glimpse of a deer, a raccoon, or some other animal that did not have an appetite for meat. The flashlight barely illuminated the trees ten feet away from her. Brynlei scanned back and forth, but saw nothing. Then, something reflected in the light. Glowing yellow eyes emerged from the trees and bounded toward her. Before she knew what was happening, two giant paws pressed into her chest and nearly knocked her over.

Brynlei prepared herself to die a painful death, to be torn apart by wolves, never to be seen again, just like Caroline. However, when she looked into the predator's eyes, she saw Ranger instead. He was wagging his tail with his tongue hanging out, as if he was having the time of his life. She pushed him off her. Bruce was probably not far behind.

Her heart pounded. She waited and listened, but heard nothing other than Ranger's panting. Maybe Bruce was not with Ranger this time. Maybe Ranger had trotted off into the woods to find something or someone. Ranger sniffed the ground and began making his way through the brush in the same direction she'd been traveling before he'd pounced on her. The dog moved with a purpose, almost as if he was tracking something. Ranger knew these woods better than she did. Brynlei followed him.

They continued, slowly but steadily, toward an unknown destination. Ranger stopped frequently to sniff the air or smell the trees, and Brynlei stayed a step behind him. They hiked for so long that she thought they must have passed the spot where she saw Caroline holding Rebel's reins. She had not ventured this deep into the woods before.

Eventually, the brush thinned out and Ranger stepped onto a narrow, dirt path. The path was not wide and groomed like Foxwoode's current marked trail system. This path must have been one of Foxwoode's old trails, one that wasn't in use anymore. A trail from before Caroline disappeared.

The moment she stepped onto the path, footsteps sounded behind her. Ranger let out a short, happy bark. Brynlei took off, sprinting along the path. She knew who was chasing her, and she wasn't about to let him catch her.

Footsteps pounded faster, closing in on her. Brynlei darted off the rocky path and squeezed between the trees, her arms outstretched to feel through the darkness. A stray branch sliced into the side of her face, but she forced her way through the brush, no longer certain which direction she was heading. She clamored down a steep embankment, her knees buckling and hands pushing away the wet earth, willing herself to get back up. The truth dangled in front of her like a low-hanging star, but the odds of her living to tell anyone about her discovery were shrinking with every footstep crashing behind her.

Just before the hands grabbed her in the dark and wrestled her to the ground, a cyclone of thoughts reeled through Brynlei's mind. Her cabin mates sleeping comfortably in their bunks. The void of Anna's absence beside her. The golden notes of music floating from Rebecca's violin. The buttery-sweet scent of her mom's oatmeal cookies baking in the oven. Her wonderfully boring life back in Franklin Corners. Lastly, she pictured each word printed in the glossy pages of the Foxwoode Riding Academy brochure and almost laughed at its false advertising, its glaring omission. Nowhere in the crisp twenty-page packet was there any mention of Caroline Watson, the fifteen-year-old girl who went out on a trail ride four years earlier. And never returned.

The hands gripped her arm and yanked her off balance. Brynlei tripped over her feet, her head bouncing off the cold, hard ground. He was on top of her. His weight pinned her body to the wet earth and his calloused hands restrained her arms. He flipped her over and leaned in close to her, his labored breath assaulting her face, his eyes clouded black with hatred.

"Why couldn't you let it be?" A large vein bulged down the middle of Bruce's forehead.

"Please," whispered Brynlei, "Don't kill me."

Bruce pulled a rope out of his pocket and yanked Brynlei to her feet before tying her wrists tightly together behind her back. Brynlei caught a glimpse of a metallic object in Bruce's hand. The razor-sharp edge of a knife reflected fleetingly in the dim light of the stars. Her knees buckled.

"Stand." Bruce yanked her up again. This time the rope cut into her wrists, burning her skin.

Terrifying thoughts consumed her mind. Was Bruce going to kill her? Or would he kidnap her and hold her captive? Torture her? Is that what happened to Caroline? Would she ever see her family? She couldn't deny the sinking feeling in her stomach. This was the end. Brynlei gasped for air and squeezed her eyes shut.

She envisioned a scene from her next life. She'd be at a dinner party, a silk dress skimming her slender curves, wavy blond hair cascading to her shoulders. She'd be laughing at a joke, clinking wine glasses with people who looked like her parents. She'd hear the name "Caroline" in a passing conversation, causing her blood to run cold. A fleeting moment of recognition would paralyze her. The crystal wine glass would slip out of her hand and shatter across the marble floor. The hostess would run to her side, insisting that the broken glass was no big deal and asking if she was feeling okay. Brynlei would have to trust her future-self to remember the truth, to grasp at a memory just out of reach.

The rope tugged at her wrists, causing her to take a few steps backward. Brynlei opened her eyes and tried to scream. Bruce was tying her to a tree.

"Please. Let me go. I won't tell anyone." Brynlei tried to make eye contact with Bruce, but he focused on tying the rope.

"Tell anyone what?" Bruce whipped around and glared directly into

Brynlei's eyes, causing her to shrink down.

"I … I don't know. I mean, if you're responsible for whatever happened to Caroline. I won't tell anyone."

"Caroline is dead. Don't you listen to the news?" Bruce's voice was angry.

"But I saw her." As soon as she said the words, Brynlei wished she could take them back.

"Well, that's a problem." Bruce stood motionless for a moment. Then he began to laugh.

The laughter came in waves, softly at first, then louder, then bellowing as if he was howling at the moon. It was the kind of laugh that could only come from a crazy person. The laughing ceased just as abruptly as it had started.

"You and your blue-haired friend couldn't leave it alone, could you? How many warnings do I have to give you? Now I have no choice." Bruce lifted the knife from his pocket once again and stepped even closer to Brynlei so that his hot breath steamed her face. The thick, moist breath dampening her skin would be the last thing she felt before the knife sliced across her throat. Brynlei heaved with fear and braced herself for whatever was coming next.

"Bruce! No!" A woman's voice shouted from a distance.

Brynlei's eyes popped open just as a woman with flowing black hair ran toward her through the trees. Even in the dark, the green eyes were unmistakable. It was Caroline.

"What are you doing?" Caroline demanded of Bruce. Caroline's forehead creased with worry as she struggled to catch her breath.

"She's gonna ruin everything. I have to stop her." Bruce waved the knife in the air.

"No. You don't need to do anything." Caroline stepped in between Bruce and Brynlei, a human shield. "We can explain everything to her. Tell her the truth. She'll have to keep our secret. Put the knife down."

"She won't believe me. She's already made up her mind."

"No, I haven't." Brynlei stared directly into Bruce's eyes. "I'll listen to everything. I can keep a secret."

"Bruce, you haven't done anything bad." Caroline outstretched her arms and grabbed his shoulders. "Don't ruin your life now by doing something that could really get you into trouble. If anything happens to her, they'll trace it back to you. They'll find me. Please."

Bruce froze like a cat watching a bird. "I guess you're right." Bruce's arms dropped to his sides. "I don't wanna hurt anyone. I was just gonna scare her off. To protect you."

"I'll keep your secret," Brynlei said again, not flinching. "I promise."

Bruce hung his head and placed the knife gently in Caroline's hand.

* * * *

Bruce pulled her along by the rope, Ranger in the lead and Caroline following behind. They walked in uncomfortable silence back to the narrow path and then veered off into the woods beyond. Five minutes, ten minutes, Brynlei wasn't sure how long she stumbled through the woods. She put one foot in front of the other and tried to imagine what they were going to tell her.

The faint light from the flashlight revealed a steep wooded hill covered by a thick blanket of leaves. A black mound rose up in front of them. Bruce leaned down and brushed aside some leaves, uncovering a wooden panel built into the side of the sloped hill.

Brynlei gasped. What was this? Bruce grasped a wooden knob and pulled up. Slowly, the door opened and a warm light radiated from within the secret hideaway.

Bruce entered the cave-like cabin first and motioned for Brynlei to follow. When Brynlei hesitated, Caroline nodded at her, letting her know it was okay. Still a sense of fear filled Brynlei's stomach like a heavy rock. She couldn't shake it.

As Brynlei carefully descended the wooden steps, the scent of cedar, flowers, raspberries, and soap swirled through her nose, reminding her of an old-fashioned general store. Ranger bounded in after Caroline with his tail wagging. Two battery-powered lights clipped to the ceiling illuminated the inside of the cabin.

Wood paneling covered the walls and ceiling. A makeshift bed, consisting of a mess of sleeping bags, blankets, and pillows covered the floor at the far end of the room. A bulletin board hung next to the bed with worn photos of horses and girls and a dog covering its surface.

Small cubbies stacked in the corner held clothes and dishes and some kind of medical kit. Built-in shelves were stocked to the hilt with cans of food, granola bars, bottled water, beef jerky, applesauce, and bowls full of fresh raspberries. Another shelf hung below a scratched mirror and held soap, shampoo, conditioner, and lotion. Brynlei's missing Tom's of Maine deodorant stood in full view on the shelf amongst the other toiletries. A small table and two wooden chairs occupied most of the space in the front room, while stacks and stacks of books, mostly dealing with veterinary medicine, lined the walls. A pinecone wreath hung above the door and garlands of dried flowers decorated the walls.

Brynlei needed a moment to absorb what she was seeing and realize she was inside Caroline's home. Despite the musty smell, the cabin had a warm energy about it, not at all like a place where someone was being held captive.

"You can sit down." Caroline gestured to one of the wooden chairs.

Caroline's nervous voice also sounded friendly, so Brynlei allowed herself to breathe for a moment.

"Are you Caroline Watson?" Brynlei already knew the answer. Who else could this striking beauty with the shiny black hair and breathtaking green eyes be?

"Yes."

"Do you know everyone is looking for you?"

"Yes, although they stopped looking for me about three and a half years ago."

"I'm sure that's not true," Brynlei said. "I'm sure your parents must be so worr—"

"It's okay," Caroline interrupted. "I don't want to be found."

"Why?"

Caroline glanced over at Bruce who stood in front of the door, blocking Brynlei's escape route. It was obvious he still didn't trust her. Bruce gave a slight nod, signaling to Caroline that he'd go along with her plan. Brynlei sat rigidly in the rickety wooden chair as Caroline began speaking.

"I guess this only makes sense if I start from the beginning." Caroline looked over at Brynlei, her eyes piercing through her.

The story that began to flow out of Caroline's mouth was beyond anything Brynlei could have imagined. If Brynlei's hands had been free, she would have written down every word Caroline spoke just so she would have proof it wasn't all a dream. The rope still cut into Brynlei's wrists so, instead, she listened. Each word out of Caroline's mouth was like a long-lost artifact being unearthed for first time in ages.

Caroline recounted how her childhood had been a happy one. She grew up modestly, an only child who lived with her parents on large piece of land outside of Lansing.

"My mother was young when she married my dad. She didn't have any education past high school, but she always said she didn't need it because my dad took care of us. She stayed home with me. Come to think of it, she even doted on me. She encouraged me to follow my dreams, probably out of a desire to make up for her own unhappy childhood." Caroline paused and looked at the floor.

"My dad was a veterinarian who ran his own practice on part of our property. He specialized in equine veterinary care. There were always at least three or four horses out back at any given time, and I was fascinated by them from as far back as I can remember. My dad used to let me sit nearby and observe as he cared for the horses and nursed their injuries, explaining everything to me along the way. I learned to ride on the horses boarded on our property. My dad taught me at first. Later, he turned my lessons over to a riding instructor who lived down the road. Her name was Betsy."

Caroline's face beamed as she recounted how Betsy had recognized, even from the time Caroline was eight or nine, that she had a special way of communicating with the horses, and how the horses, even the "difficult" ones, wanted to please her.

"I had a pony named Pistachio. His owners abandoned him at my dad's vet clinic after not being able to pay the bill. They called Pistachio an obstinate old mule. Said he wasn't worth the money. I begged my dad not put Pistachio down, to let me keep him. It didn't take long for him to agree. After just a few months of training, we were competing in the hunters and bringing home ribbons. He was a special pony.

"It's funny to think back on how perfect my life seemed at that time." Caroline paused, her green eyes piercing into Brynlei. "Then, how quickly it all came crashing down.

"When I was twelve, my dad was shot to death, just because he was in the wrong place at the wrong time. He went into the Mobile station to pay for a tank of gas and never came out. He got caught up in a scuffle between some guys robbing the place and the owner. The police arrived a couple minutes after my dad. They started shooting and hit my dad in the crossfire. They said he died instantly."

Brynlei remembered back to the article she'd seen online about Caroline's dad being shot. Caroline continued speaking, as if in a trance.

"After losing my dad I thought my life couldn't get any worse, but it did. My mother changed after that. Or maybe it just revealed her true personality. Six months after dad died, my mother started dating Steve McDaniel, one of the police officers who'd been at the Mobile station that day. Steve always claimed he wasn't the one who fired the shot that killed my dad, but I didn't trust him."

Caroline explained how she became more and more disgusted with her mother for betraying her dad so blatantly. Her mother would leave Caroline alone for hours at night and stumble in drunk at one. Eventually, her mother and Steve would stumble in drunk and not emerge from the bedroom until morning.

"I couldn't understand my mother's attraction to Steve. I could not find a single redeeming quality in him, except maybe for being the best liar I had ever met."

Caroline laughed, but her the corners of her mouth turned down.

"Spending time with my pony and my dog, Tulip, was the only thing that made me feel better. Taking care of my animals and training for horse shows gave me something else to focus on. While I was busy with my animals, my friends moved on. The girls who used to be my friends started ridiculing me. By the time I turned fourteen, the few friends I still had were totally boy crazy, but the boys weren't looking at them, they were looking at me. I didn't want the attention, but it always came my way. Betsy told me I was "blossoming" in all the right places. I guess my friends viewed me as a liability.

"Girls at school spread rumors about me. Horrible things that weren't true. They stopped talking to me in the hallways and inviting me to their houses. I decided it was less painful to be alone. I guess it was the only way I could think of to protect myself." Caroline crossed her arms in front of her chest and glanced at the photos on her bulletin board.

"Pistachio and Tulip were my only true friends. My animals were loyal, and I knew they wouldn't betray me. I decided I wanted to be a veterinarian like my dad. I'd spend hours inside my dad's old clinic, pretending to treat imaginary injuries on Pistachio and Tulip, keeping notes of everything my dad had taught me so I wouldn't forget. I studied his veterinary journals, even though most of the information was over my head.

"My mother married Steve two weeks after my fourteenth birthday. She forced me to stand next to her and Steve and smile during the ceremony, even though I was screaming on the inside. I could smell the alcohol on Steve's breath and I prayed for someone to object to the marriage, to stop the ceremony, but no one did. It wasn't long before Steve took charge of our finances and told me there would be no more money for my "pony rides" and definitely not for horse shows. I was devastated and I begged my mother to take my side, to do something. She was so pathetic. She let Steve ruin our lives."

Brynlei shook her head. She couldn't imagine a mother treating her child so carelessly, especially after she'd lost her dad.

Caroline continued riding whenever she could, either with Pistachio in the back yard or at Betsy's barn down the road. She earned a little money from people who would pay her to help train their horses or ride their horses while they were on vacation, but it wasn't enough to pay for horse shows. It definitely wasn't enough to attend Foxwoode.

Betsy was the one who insisted Caroline apply for a scholarship. She told Caroline that Foxwoode paid all expenses for one deserving horsewoman every summer and there was no reason why it couldn't be her. Caroline saw it as a chance to improve her riding and to escape from Steve and her mother, if only for three weeks.

"I filled out the application and hand-delivered it to the post office myself. I think I ran out to the mailbox every day after that. I couldn't wait to hear back from Foxwoode. I tried to spend as little time as possible in the house with my mother and Steve. He enjoyed picking on me and accusing me of being a spoiled, little brat who was too pretty for my own good. He was always staring at me, grabbing me in improper places, and then laughing it off. He made me uncomfortable being in my own house. I was so angry with my mother for ignoring the way Steve acted toward me."

Caroline sifted the ends of her hair through her fingers as she recounted how she caught Steve staring at her one morning as she left for school. He said, "I'll need to buy a bigger shotgun to keep all the boys away." He forced her to give him a hug before she left the house. She tried to give him a quick hug just so she could get out of there, but Steve wouldn't let go. His hands slipped down too low and Caroline couldn't get away.

"A father doesn't hug his daughter like that." Caroline's voice was laced with hatred. "I began locking my bedroom door at night, afraid that a drunk Steve would decide to pay me a visit, but Steve surprised me. He attacked me during the day, when I didn't expect it."

Brynlei drew in a sharp breath. She didn't like where this was going. All of the sudden, she felt ridiculous for ever complaining about her parents.

Caroline stared at the floor as she described how Steve came home from work early in the afternoon, drunk as usual. Her mother was working at her new part-time job organizing files for a dental office. Caroline spoke in a calm and even voice, as if giving a weather report.

"Steve grabbed me by the neck, choking me as he ripped my skirt off. I saw him unbuckling his belt and I freaked out. I knew what he was going to do. There was a pen on the side table next to my head, so I reached up and grabbed it. Then I plunged it into his back over and over. The pen didn't do anything except startle him, but he reached back to grab it out of my hand. That's when I kneed him as hard as I could. He doubled over in pain.

"I guess I stunned him. I saw my opportunity to get away, so I ran to the kitchen and grabbed the biggest knife I could find. It took every ounce of will power I had not to kill him. He looked up, and when he saw me with the knife, he started laughing uncontrollably. He said 'What are you going to do? Kill me? Killing a police officer isn't a very smart thing to do.' I told him to get up and leave. Then his laughter stopped and his face turned to stone.

"He looked me in the eyes and threatened to torture and kill my animals if I ever dreamed of mentioning any of it to my mother or anyone else. 'Anyway,' he told me, 'no one would believe you. Always remember, I'm a police officer and you're just a dumb little slut.' Then he laughed, grabbed a pop out of the refrigerator, and went back to work as if nothing had happened."

Brynlei stared at Caroline. Speechless.

"I kept Steve's attack a secret for over three months." Caroline fixed her gaze on her lap. "It was the worst three months of my life. Everything became a struggle: sleeping, eating, breathing. Even riding was difficult. The burden of keeping the secret felt like it was crushing me. I constantly worried Steve would attack me again. I lay awake at night envisioning how I'd defend myself better the next time.

"Then one night, Pistachio died in his sleep. His death crushed me, but I only let myself cry in front of Betsy. My mother said she could tell I was depressed. She gave me a half-hearted hug and told me that it was for the best, that Steve wouldn't have let me keep Pistachio much longer anyway because of the expense. Then, I pretty much lost it."

Caroline described the wave of emotion that crashed over her and pulled her mother down in its undertow. She yelled and cried and screamed at her mother about what a fool she was to marry Steve. That Steve had probably shot her dad. That Steve had tried to force himself on her three months earlier and threatened her if she told anyone.

"For a second, I thought I saw a glint of understanding in my mother's eyes. That maybe she would finally come to her senses and kick Steve out of the house, divorce him."

Instead, Caroline's mother's arm reached back and swung at her face. The smack stung Caroline's cheek, but more than that, it stunned her. Her mother had never hit her before. She called Caroline a jealous liar and a slut and screamed at her to never talk about Steve like that again. Caroline couldn't believe it. She had nowhere to turn.

"That night I hid in my bedroom with Tulip while my mother and Steve watched a movie on the couch in the living room. I could make out some muffled talking that grew angry at one point and then turned to laughter. My mother had completely abandoned and betrayed me.

"I thought about taking Tulip and running away, but I didn't know where to go. I knew Betsy would believe me, but I didn't want to put her or her horses in danger."

Caroline described how she cried herself to sleep, feeling hopeless and alone. There was no way she could have known that the worst hadn't happened yet.

"The next morning, I woke up to brakes screeching outside my window and Steve swearing. Somehow, I knew that something horrible had just happened. Tulip wasn't on my bed. Someone had let her out. I ran out to the driveway in my bare feet and nightgown and found Tulip crushed under the tires of Steve's police car. I tried to help her, but it was obvious it was too late. I lost control.

"I knew Steve had done it on purpose, that he was punishing me for telling my mother what had happened. I lunged at him and started hitting him and screaming at him, calling him a murderer and a child molester. It shouldn't have been a surprise, but my mother yelled at me. She came to Steve's defense when she should have been comforting me. Steve kept saying how he hadn't seen the dog behind his car until it was too late. 'It was an accident,' he said over and over again, trying to apologize to me. He should have won an Oscar for his acting. I almost believed him myself." Tears appeared in the corners of Caroline's eyes as she spoke.

Just as her mother went inside to find some towels, Steve smirked at Caroline, letting her know that it wasn't at all an accident. He would not let her win.

The days that followed were the darkest of Caroline's life. She had no friends, her beloved pets were dead, her stepfather terrified her, and her mother had betrayed her. Caroline stopped herself from turning to Betsy, for fear Steve would kill her animals as well. Thoughts of ending it all and joining her dad in heaven stuck in Caroline's brain. The only thing that kept her going was the hope of being accepted to Foxwoode and escaping her miserable existence for a few weeks. Three days after Tulip was killed, as if her dad was helping her from up above, Caroline opened the mailbox to find a letter from Foxwoode Riding Academy. The letter congratulated her for being selected as the recipient of Foxwoode's summer scholarship.

"Steve agreed I could go, only because it didn't cost him anything. I survived the next few months by dreaming of Foxwoode. I dreamed that Foxwoode's owners would notice my riding abilities and ask me to work for them, even though I knew I was too young. I dreamed that I would make friends. I dreamed that somehow, while I was there, I'd figure out a way to escape from my life."

After Caroline's mother and Steve dropped her at Foxwoode, Caroline watched from the steps of the cabin as their car sped away in a cloud of exhaust and dust. It had been one of the happiest moments of her life. She felt safe for the first time since her dad died.

Brynlei remembered how much she had missed her parents when they drove away in a cloud of dust two weeks ago, how she had almost screamed for them to come back. She couldn't fathom how sad Caroline's life must have been.

Brynlei wanted to reach over and hug Caroline, but her hands were still tied, so she sat motionless as Caroline continued her story.

Caroline's riding had excelled at Foxwoode. She was assigned a spirited young mare named Sally, who needed training over fences. The Olsons knew about Caroline's talent for training horses and hoped she could perform her magic with Sally. Caroline worked patiently with the nervous mare, rewarding her for even the smallest efforts until, after only two weeks, she guided Sally over a course of eight fences, complete with flying lead changes, no bucking, and no refusals. The Olsons were ecstatic with Sally's progress and Caroline got the feeling she was going to win Top Rider.

"At first, I had an easier time making friends at Foxwoode, maybe because there were no boys around. Then, after a while, it seemed like the other girls were jealous of all the praise I was getting for my riding. I tried to downplay everything and made a point to compliment the other girls on their riding, but they started going to the beach or leaving for trail rides without me. As much as I didn't want to let them affect me, it hurt. I realized no matter how hard I tried, I would never fit in."

It was during a trail ride with Miss Catherine, her Foxwoode riding instructor, that Caroline came up with the idea to disappear. Caroline's eyes sparkled as she remembered the first time she and Miss Catherine took the unmarked trail deep into the woods.

"It was as if the trees enveloped me, the walls of the forest protecting me from all sides. I felt at peace. I knew that no one could hurt me or bother me or betray me out here. I could just be myself and I could finally breathe. I thought, 'I can do this. I can finally escape from my life and create a new reality for myself.' I had read about people living off the grid, away from all the pressures of society, and I became obsessed with the idea. Of course, I didn't realize how difficult it would be to do it on my own." Caroline glanced at Bruce.

"Two days before my last day at Foxwoode, I was alone in the cabin. The other girls had left for the beach while I was in the bathroom. It was obvious they were trying to ditch me. When I realized they'd left without me, it stung. I guess it was the straw that broke the camel's back. I decided that would be the last time I'd let other people hurt me. I was going do it, escape from the world of humans and live in the wilderness. I'd studied the map of Foxwoode and the surrounding forest and located a remote spot nearly four miles north where I planned to camp the first night. I took a small bag and loaded it with some things I thought I'd need to escape and survive in the woods—my Swiss Army knife, a compass, a lighter, twine, plastic bags, Band-Aids, a change of clothes, my moccasin slippers, a few photos of Pistachio and Tulip, as many granola bars as I could carry, and a couple bottles of water. I made sure to leave most of my valuables behind so no one got the impression I was running away. I also made sure to leave my helmet behind." Caroline continued talking, as if in a trance.

"After I made the decision to leave, I felt like someone else was controlling my body. I found myself at the barn tacking up Sally. She could feel my nervousness and she pranced around while I tightened her girth and fastened her bridle. When I was sure no one was watching, I trotted her to the trailhead and guided her to the first unmarked trail I could find. The path twisted and turned through the woods, but eventually I found a way to head north. I couldn't stop myself from crying as we meandered through the forest, but I was happy, too. I tried to enjoy the ride because I knew it might be the last time I would ever ride a horse.

"When Sally and I were a good mile and half north of the barn, I decided it was time. We'd reached a perfect spot, near the deep, rocky river, but still close enough to the barn that Sally could find her way back. I slid off her back and loosened the girth a couple holes so the saddle turned sideways. I wanted everyone to think that I'd fallen into the river in an accident and drowned. I yelled at Sally to go home, but she just looked at me with her big, brown eyes. She wouldn't leave me. Finally, I had no choice but to grab a stick off the ground and swing it at her. Sally was confused and continued to follow me. I felt horrible, like now I was the one who was doing the betraying. But I kept up the swinging and she eventually trotted away. I prayed that it wouldn't be long until someone found her wandering and led her back to safety. I prayed that her legs would not get tripped up in the dangling reins."

Caroline paused and took a deep breath. Brynlei guessed that shooing Sally away four years ago still affected her.

"When Sally was out of sight, I knew I didn't have much time until someone found her and started looking for me. I staged the scene of my accident. I used my knife to slice my finger open. I made sure to get plenty of blood on my boot and on some jagged rocks near the river's edge. Then I threw my boot in the river. I even pulled out some of my hair and wedged it in the crack between two rocks. I wanted there to be no doubt that I fell off my horse, hit my head on a rock, and drowned in the river. With the rushing current and the rocky bottom, I knew it would be nearly impossible for anyone to dredge. I bandaged up my finger and slipped on my moccasins, so as not to leave a trail of any kind—no blood, no footprints. Then, I ran as fast as I could in the other direction, heading north for what must have been two hours. I slid off my moccasins three different times as I crossed streams. If they used dogs to track me, I wanted to throw them off my scent.

"At first, food was not an issue. I was too nervous to eat anything. Every time I heard a noise in the woods, I thought someone was about to find me, to ruin my plan. At one point, I heard people calling my name in the distance so I climbed up the branches of an enormous pine tree, hiding and waiting up above. It seemed like I was up there for hours before the voices grew fainter and eventually disappeared.

"The first few nights, I barely slept. I was petrified of being found. I knew Steve was probably out looking for me and making a big show out of it. If he was trying to find me it was only because he wanted to make sure I didn't tell anyone what had happened. I could only imagine what he'd do to me the next time.

"I made a bed of pine needles under that huge tree. I figured it was easy to climb straight up if I heard anyone coming, but the nights terrified me. The noises were unfamiliar and it was so pitch black I could not see my hand in front of my face. Even wearing my sweatshirt, I was cold. It made me wonder how I would survive the winter. Aside from the weather, I knew there were coyotes and bears in these woods and I didn't have a plan on how to defend myself, if it ever came to that. I was determined to stick to my plan. I decided I needed to build a shelter of some kind. Obviously, it would have to be hidden.

"I spent nearly two days roaming the area on the map where I thought I'd be least likely to be found. I'd eaten all of my granola bars by that point. I was hungry and exhausted. Finally, I spotted a rocky hill, dense with trees. The roots of a large tree formed a hollow indentation in the side of the hill. If I curled up in a ball, I could fit in it. I stacked a pile of sticks, rocks, and leaves in front of the opening to keep hidden. That hole in the hill became my home for the next ten days. The wild raspberries and stream water kept me alive.

"Even though I was hungry and the nights were cold, I loved lying inside the tree and looking up at the stars. I had never seen stars shine so bright before." Caroline face lit up, as she looked at Brynlci. "I know it seems like I should have been lonely and missing something from home, but I wasn't. I only missed my dad and Tulip and Pistachio, and I pretended they were up in the stars looking down on me, but I guess it wasn't as great of a hiding place as I thought." Caroline smiled at Bruce, as if embarrassed. "That's where Bruce found me."

Brynlei gasped and swung her head toward Bruce. So he had found her in the woods four years ago and never turned her in? Never told anyone? Brynlei's eyes begged Bruce for answers, for an explanation.

This time it was Bruce who spoke. "I found her on pure luck. I brought Ranger out here for trainin'. Always figured he'd make a good huntin' dog. He never did take to huntin', but he led me right to her." Bruce patted Ranger on the head and stared at the floor.

"She looked near death. I knew right away who she was, even though she was asleep and covered in dirt. I nudged her and said, 'It's gonna be alright.' She looked up at me as if she'd seen a ghost. She started cryin' and beggin' me not to tell anyone where she was. I told her these woods were no place for a girl. She'd die out here, I knew that much. I told her I'd take her back. Her skinny arms were shiverin' with cold, so I figured she'd agree, but she kept beggin' me not to tell, to just go away. She must have said it a hundred times. Finally, I asked what could possibly be so bad that she'd rather starve and freeze out here than go home. Then she told me the same story you just heard." Bruce shook his head and cleared his throat.

"I felt bad about all the hard luck she'd seen. I told her she could go to the authorities, that I'd back her up, but she said Steve *was* the authorities, and that her own mother didn't believe her. She would not go back to her life. Not until she was at least eighteen and could be on her own. I figured I didn't blame her much. It wasn't my place to bring more heartache into her life. If her story was true, they'd put her in a foster home. I lived with foster parents when I was a teenager and I can tell you, it ain't fun."

Bruce paused and fidgeted his hands.

"Whether it was right or not, I told her I'd help her survive out here. I figured she wasn't too different from me—no family and no friends to speak of. Of course, I have my aunt and uncle to help me out, but Caroline didn't have anyone. First thing I did was bring her food and water. I snuck out every night, starting right after dinner, and worked on buildin' her a proper shelter. I worked on it every chance I got, which wasn't easy what with all the searches goin' on and the media about. By that point, though, they had pretty much presumed her dead. She'd thrown those old boys off with the bloody boot in the river and her blood and hair on the rock. They figured she must've drowned. That was one thing she did right." Bruce shot Caroline a look of approval.

Brynlei remembered Alyssa's comment about the police being stupid and smiled in spite of herself.

"It took a solid week, but we dug out this room where you're sittin' now. Caroline worked just as hard as me. Then I finished the inside with plaster and scrap wood that was left over from the repairs to the main barn. I hauled the supplies out in the middle of the night. By the time we finished the door, you couldn't even tell this place was here. I finally got to use my construction background for somethin' worthwhile."

"But how do you survive out here in the winter? Even with this shelter," Brynlei asked.

"Bruce brings me supplies whenever he can. I have a battery-powered space heater and a propane burner for cooking food. He raids the Lost and Found after the girls leave each session and tells the Olsons he's taking the things to the Salvation Army. Then he brings me all the clothes, blankets, books, and shoes people leave behind. I have everything I need right here. Bruce brings me extra food from the kitchen, too." Caroline nodded to her shelf of canned goods. "In the summer, I pick the wild raspberries. I made a mistake this year and wandered too close to the trail. That's when you saw me the first time."

Brynlei didn't know if she should correct Caroline. She was now certain she'd already seen Caroline twice before that. The first time was when her parents took a wrong turn onto the service road and the second time she'd spotted Caroline across the lake the night of the bonfire.

"I made a mistake when you saw me the next time, too," Caroline said. "That beautiful chestnut horse was galloping through the woods with the reins dangling down. He reminded me so much of Sally. I couldn't let him get tangled up and hurt himself. I thought I could untangle him and take off before anyone saw me, but then you were there."

"Has anyone else seen you?" Brynlei asked. "I mean, they must have. Over all these years."

"Yes, I've been spotted a few times, mostly by hikers who've gone off the trails in the State Forest. Thankfully, they didn't know who I was. I pretended to be staying at Foxwoode each time and said I was on a day hike. They didn't question me. Of course, I took off before they could get a good look at me." Caroline hesitated before she continued. "Bruce built secret doors in the floors of a couple of the cabins. He and I use them sometimes to get supplies without anyone knowing. I guess you'd call it stealing, but we didn't really have a choice." Caroline smiled, but her eyes glistened with sadness.

Brynlei wanted to tell Caroline she had found the door in Cabin 5 yesterday, but she kept it to herself.

"Then there was the girl who saw me in her cabin at night. Bruce had broken his leg two summers ago and couldn't make it out to bring me supplies. I thought something had happened to him, that he'd been fired, or left me. I found him in his cabin at night with a cast on his leg and he explained the situation, said he wouldn't be able to bring me supplies for another month. I desperately needed soap and shampoo and couldn't wait that long, so I snuck in through the door in the floor of the cabin. I should have stayed in the bathroom, but I just wanted to see their faces, to see what young girls filled with hope looked like. Then, a girl woke up and saw me standing over her bed. She looked terrified and quickly closed her eyes. I bolted back out the secret door, so by the time she opened her eyes again, I was gone. Bruce told me rumors started swirling around that I was a ghost who came back to haunt Foxwoode." Caroline laughed, like that was the stupidest idea she'd ever heard. Brynlei's cheeks flushed in embarrassment.

"Did you come in our cabin and take my deodorant?" Brynlei asked. She had so many questions she didn't know why she started with the least important one.

"No. Sorry, I didn't know I had your deodorant." Caroline followed Brynlei's line of vision to the deodorant sitting on the shelf. "Bruce usually gets all the supplies and brings them out to me."

Brynlei began to understand Bruce's anger toward her when she stayed back in the cabin while all the other girls went to the beach. She must have interfered with him getting supplies for Caroline.

"But how do you shower? And where do you go to the bathroom?" Brynlei was still trying to wrap her head around how someone could survive in the woods for four years.

"I bathe in the stream or the river when it's warm out. In the winter, I have to melt the ice on my little stove. When it got down to thirty-five degrees below zero last winter, Bruce let me stay in the Olson's house for two days. He lives there in the winter while the Olsons are in Florida. Occasional workmen and delivery people came by though, so it was risky." Caroline smiled. "I dig holes to go to the bathroom, like campers. Then I cover it up. It's not glamorous, but it works."

"Are you going to stay out here forever?" Brynlei asked.

"No. That's the thing," Caroline said. "I'm over eighteen now. Steve died eight months ago. I don't have to hide out here anymore. I'm going to start my new life in a few weeks, in North Carolina. Bruce is helping me create a new identity and start fresh. The paperwork is almost ready. Just a few more weeks."

"But how—" Brynlei started.

"I've got friends in low places," Bruce said, smiling wryly. "I paid a guy every penny I've ever saved to get a social security number for a nineteen year-old girl named Jane Carlisle."

"That's going to be my name," Caroline said. "But if people find me hiding out here now, these past four years will have been for nothing."

Brynlei suddenly understood the enormity of her discovery. The terrible timing and the threat she must be posing to Caroline's future.

"But if you're over eighteen and Steve is dead, why do you need a fake identity?"

"I tricked the police. We tricked the police." Caroline corrected herself. "It's a serious crime. We could face jail time. If I have to pay for what I've done, that's one thing, but I'm not bringing Bruce down with me. He saved my life."

Brynlei thought of Anna being framed and unfairly sent home, of Anna's teddy bear hanging with its eyes gauged out. She had suspected Bruce was behind it, but now she knew why. She actually understood. Brynlei and Anna had been getting too close to discovering Caroline's secret, of finding out the truth, just weeks before Caroline was to be free to start her new life. Their discovery would have sent Bruce and Caroline to jail instead. She didn't blame Bruce for doing what was necessary. She was relieved that her initial instincts about Bruce had been correct. He was a good person. She hadn't lost her ability to sense people's character after all.

"But how did you know Anna and I were looking for Caroline?" Brynlei looked at Bruce.

"A couple weeks ago, I overheard you tellin' Anna that you saw Caroline on the trail, when Rebel bucked you off."

Brynlei's face turned a deep shade of red. So Bruce had been there all along. He'd seen and heard everything.

"Then I saw you girls ridin' off the trail a few days later and I knew you wouldn't leave it alone. I feel real bad about scarin' Anna and sendin' her home, but I had to protect Caroline." Bruce shook his head, and his eyelids drooped like a sad dog.

Brynlei's instincts about the bear and the alcohol had been right.

"Then I found your red notebook with the map. You circled the exact location of this cabin. That's when I knew I had to come out here and stop you."

Brynlei gasped. They hadn't known the cabin was here. Would they have been able to find it? It was well-hidden, built into the hill and covered under the leaves. Perhaps she and Anna had been even closer to finding Caroline than they realized.

"What will you do in North Carolina?" Brynlei said, still struggling to absorb this new reality.

"I've been taking correspondence classes under my new name—Jane Carlisle." Caroline pointed to the stacks of folders and books that lined her walls. "Bruce brings me all the materials. I earned my GED and I've completed another class that certifies me as a veterinary assistant. Bruce also brings me veterinary supplies from the animal shelter. So I can practice. Not on real animals, just for pretend. I still want to go to college someday and become a real veterinarian."

"If you can live in the woods for four years, you can probably do anything," Brynlei said.

The underground cabin filled with an awkward silence. Caroline smiled.

"I'm sorry about your friend, Anna, getting sent home. Bruce only did what he needed to do to protect me. She was a good rider. I saw her from the woods the other day."

"You never should've been over there," Bruce said, shaking his head.

"No one has ever seen me from that spot before. It's completely hidden." Caroline turned toward Brynlei. "I watch one lesson toward the end of each session to see if I can guess who will be Top Rider. Bruce thinks it's dangerous for me to get so close. I thought Anna deserved it this year."

Brynlei nodded in agreement. There was nothing she could do about the wrong that had been done to Anna. Clearing Anna's name would mean risking Caroline's future.

"How did you see me back there?" Caroline asked.

"Sometimes I sense things other people miss," Brynlei said. "I sensed your presence. I could feel you watching. I saw your eyes. Then I saw your footprints in the mud."

"Before I covered 'em up," Bruce said.

All the pieces of the puzzle had fallen into place. Brynlei finally understood everything that she had seen and heard and felt the last two and a half weeks. Her heart ached for Caroline, yet she was in awe of Caroline's strength at the same time. She admired Bruce for doing the right thing, despite putting himself at risk. More than anything, she wanted Caroline to move on with her life, to succeed, and follow her dreams. Brynlei would not be the one responsible for sending Caroline to jail. Or Bruce, for that matter.

"Your secret is safe with me." Brynlei focused on Caroline's impossibly green eyes as she said the words. Caroline nodded. Brynlei looked at Bruce. "Yours, too. I'll never tell anyone. Not even Anna."

She meant it. Her word was good, but her stomach lurched at the thought of betraying Anna to save Caroline. She'd have to choose the lesser of the two evils and tell Anna she hadn't been able to find out anything.

"It's time we get you back to your cabin." Bruce cut off the rope that bound Brynlei's wrists. "The girls will be waking up soon."

Chapter Fifteen

The alarm jarred her awake. How could it be time to get up already? Rays of sunlight beamed in through the window, stabbing Brynlei's eyes. Her legs and arms felt as if they were stuck in wet cement and her eyes refused to open. She could not pull back the covers. These were the consequences of getting less than two hours of sleep.

"Seriously, Brynlei, you need to get up and dressed." Kaitlyn's voice was even more chipper than usual. "You're going to miss breakfast."

"I'm not feeling very well." The words came out dry and hoarse. "I'm going to stay in bed."

Brynlei did not want to miss one of the last lessons before the horse show, but she couldn't force her body to move. Her mind was thick and clouded. Nothing good could come from riding in her impaired state.

"I'll tell Miss Jill," Kaitlyn said. "Can I bring you anything from the mess hall?"

"No, thanks." Brynlei just wanted to be left alone. She needed time to sleep and absorb what she'd learned last night.

"What happened to your face?" Kaitlyn took a step back. Brynlei's hand shot up to the scratch on her cheek where the branch had sliced her. It still seemed like a dream.

"Oh, I accidentally ran into the bathroom door last night." Brynlei rolled over, hiding the scratch.

"This isn't because of Anna leaving, is it?" Alyssa said. "She isn't worth it."

"Leave me alone." There was a sharp edge to Brynlei's voice that she wouldn't have dared to use with Alyssa a few days ago, but now she

152

didn't care. She knew more than Alyssa and her knowledge empowered her. She pulled the covers over her head and willed all of the girls to disappear, especially Alyssa.

When the last girl had zipped up her riding boots and slammed the wooden door, Brynlei drifted in and out of sleep. Every time she opened her eyes, it took her a minute to remember why she was in bed and what she'd discovered the previous night.

She replayed Caroline's story in her mind and struggled to comprehend the pain Caroline had endured. She saw something of herself in Caroline. She understood why Caroline wanted to escape into the forest and disappear.

Brynlei knew what it felt like to be judged, to not fit in. Yet she couldn't imagine what it would be like not to have any friends or family that she could trust. It must have been a relief for Caroline to isolate herself, the shelter of the forest protecting her from the cruelty of the world.

What would have happened to Caroline if Bruce and Ranger hadn't stumbled across her just days after she disappeared? Surely, she would have died or been forced to turn herself in come winter. Bruce must have enjoyed helping Caroline. It gave him a purpose, not to mention a friend. Or maybe Bruce was in love with Caroline, like all the other men— although she did not get that sense from him. It was more like a brother-sister relationship. What would Bruce do when Caroline left? Would he be lonely? Would he keep in touch with her? Surely, he would.

Brynlei decided to write down her phone number, email, and home address for Caroline, so that she could keep in touch. She never wanted Caroline to feel alone again. Or would that be too risky? Caroline had never asked for Brynlei to find her in the first place.

It was hard to believe that in two days, she would go back home to Franklin Corners. She would have to keep the secret from everyone, even Rebecca. Even Anna. She had looked into Caroline's hauntingly beautiful eyes and promised not to tell. She'd given her word. In a few weeks, Caroline would be long gone, off to start her new life as Jane Carlisle, and no one would ever know what had happened to Caroline Watson.

* * * *

Brynlei couldn't have asked for a nicer day for the horse show. The morning sun illuminated Foxwoode's grounds, warming her back as she prepared Jett for the ring. A gentle breeze drifted through the trees, causing the flowers in front of the jumps to sway back and forth like laughing children. There was so much to do—packing up belongings, grooming Jett, polishing boots, memorizing courses—that the morning quickly morphed into afternoon. The sun's rays embraced the families as they trickled through Foxwoode's gates to watch their daughters and sisters ride before taking them home.

An hour before the show, a buzz of rumors began to swirl through the barn about a tragic horse trailer accident near Traverse City. A dozen top-level show horses were feared injured or killed. Brynlei worried for the horses involved and felt for their owners, although she did not know many of the details. The accident was a reminder that anything could change on the flip of a coin, even for people who swam in money.

Miss Jill encouraged the girls to focus on their show, which would start at one o'clock, as planned. After the younger riders completed their classes, the Flying Foxes would compete against each other in two hunter classes and two equitation classes. While Debbie Olson and the riding instructors had likely already selected the Top Rider, they insisted a final decision would not be made until after the show when they would announce the winner.

There was a half-hour window before the show for the girls to reunite with their families. Alyssa's parents were one of the first to arrive. Brynlei watched from behind the knotty wood wall of the grooming stall as the enormous black Hummer tore past the makeshift parking lot and created its own space directly next to the barn. Alyssa's mom bounced out of the passenger door toward her daughter. High-pitched squeals tore through Brynlei's ears.

"Where's dad?" Alyssa asked her mom.

"He's trying to call work, but can't get any reception out here. Don't bother him."

Alyssa's face fell. From the Hummer's half-open window, a deep voice spewed obscenities, tarnishing the bright energy of the day.

The familiar hum of her parents' Ford Explorer reached Brynlei's ears even before she saw it. She ran toward the parking lot, as the SUV pulled off the dusty road into a marked space. Brynlei swallowed and squinted back the tears that began to form. She had never appreciated her parents more as they emerged from the car, smiling widely at her. She had missed their perfect surface lives of manicured yards, baked goods, and church socials, never having to dig deeper to dwell on all the horrendous truths that lay beneath. To her surprise, Derek popped out of the back seat and engulfed her in a bear hug. She breathed in the musty pinecone and cinnamon scent of his hair and felt like she was home.

"She's still alive," Derek said, joking with their parents. "It's been horrible without you. I've had no one to harass for three whole weeks."

She moved on to her parents, squeezing them tightly, still trying not to cry. Could they tell she was hiding something? Was it obvious she was protecting a fragile secret from being discovered?

Brynlei answered all their eager questions as honestly as she could, only lying by omission.

"We'll be cheering for you and Jett from the bleachers, honey," her mom said when it was time for Brynlei to return to the barn. "And I brought a batch of caramel butterscotch cookies for you and all your friends." Brynlei already knew about the cookies. She could smell the brown sugar, oats, eggs, butterscotch, and caramel, even from outside the car.

"Good luck, Bryn," her dad said. "Don't fall on your head."

❊ ❊ ❊ ❊

Brynlei sat tall in the saddle as she and Jett trotted into the ring for the 3' Hunter class. They'd performed well in the warm-up class. She was the fourth to go on course, and so far, no one before her had finished without issues. Kaitlyn and Daisey went first and chipped in before two of the jumps. Julia had just completed her round and trotted out of the gate on Devon, who looked wild with the whites of his eyes showing and his tail swishing vigorously. Some horses didn't respond well to the pressure of a show, or know what to do with the vibes of a nervous rider, and Devon appeared to be one of those horses.

Brynlei wanted Julia to do well, but she appeared slightly out of control aboard Devon today. They'd started smoothly, but continued to pick up speed as they went, tearing down the line in four strides instead of five. Brynlei observed Julia's mistakes and learned from them. She had to hold Jett steady down the line.

Despite sleeping through the lesson two days ago, Brynlei's lesson yesterday was smooth and focused. She needed to perform her best in the ring to prove to herself she could win, to ensure Alyssa didn't emerge victorious, and to show her parents they hadn't wasted their money on her. Even more than that, she wanted to bring home the blue ribbon for Anna. If Anna were here, she would have given Brynlei a run for her money.

Miss Jill leaned against the fence at the end of the ring, giving Brynlei last-minute tips in a hushed voice.

"Keep your eyes looking ahead. Use your corners. Don't rush. Let the oxer come to you."

Brynlei inhaled deeply, organized her reins, and trotted Jett into the ring. She held her position as she bent Jett slightly to the inside and closed her outside leg to ask for the canter. Jett picked up the correct lead immediately, as if to say, "Don't worry, Brynlei. I got this." He seemed eager to show off in front of the crowd.

She counted strides to the first fence, a white gate adorned with blue flowers, one, two, three. They found the perfect distance and Brynlei sent Jett straight to the corner before bending him toward the next line. Now she shifted her weight back in the saddle and supported his body with her outside leg to approach the line straight and at an even pace. Jett grew strong after the next jump, and Brynlei had to sit up and hold him back to fit in an even five strides down the line. Jett responded nicely.

After the line, she had a chance to get organized in the corner before approaching the enormous yellow and green oxer. Brynlei sat up through the corner and steadied Jett's pace. From three strides out, she saw their distance and waited for it. They flew over the wide jump in textbook form, Jett with his knees tucked in tight, Brynlei flexing her heels down, holding on with her calves, keeping her eyes up, and arching her back over the jump. Just three more jumps.

Next, the broken line. Brynlei organized in the corner again before approaching the stone gate jump. As they jumped it, she guided Jett straight for three strides then bent him left toward the jump with the laughing flowers. They completed the broken line in six smooth strides and now circled back to the right for the last jump—the hay bales. She steadied Jett. It was easy to rush to the last jump and miss a good distance. One, two, three. They sailed over the jump. Brynlei circled once at the end of the ring and then trotted out the gate with clapping hands and cheering voices bouncing off her ears.

"Nice ride, Brynlei," Miss Jill said, her eyes smiling.

Some of the other girls came over to congratulate her as she dismounted. Even Alyssa offered a token "Good job, Brynlei." Brynlei didn't know if she'd just won the blue ribbon, but she couldn't have done it any better than that.

The Top Rider award would likely go to Alyssa now that Anna wasn't here, but Brynlei was proud of herself and Jett for rising to the occasion. Her parents watched her from the bleachers, smiling and waving. Derek caught her gaze and gave her a double thumbs-up. Two rows below her parents sat Bruce, blending in as a casual observer. No doubt he was there to report back all the details of the show to Caroline, to tell her who had won Top Rider this year. Selfishly, Brynlei wondered if Bruce would tell Caroline about her flawless ride. Hopefully, he would.

She dismounted and held Jett's reins in her hand as Alyssa and Bentley trotted into the ring. Alyssa glanced over to the bleachers where her mom sat watching behind oversized, diamond-studded sunglasses. Beside Alyssa's mom was an empty space on the bleachers. Apparently, her dad's business call would take priority over watching his daughter ride. Brynlei saw an unfamiliar look in Alyssa's face. Disappointment? Sadness? For a moment, she almost felt sorry for Alyssa.

She felt a sudden urge to barge into Foxwoode's office and scream at Alyssa's dad to hang up the precious phone and watch his daughter for five minutes. After all, Alyssa had been working hard to prepare for this moment, just like the rest of them.

Bentley picked up a forward canter and Alyssa circled him toward the first jump. They cleared it perfectly. As they rode into the corner, Alyssa's eyes wandered back to the bleachers when she should have been looking ahead to the next jump. Alyssa and Bentley drifted out close to the rail before recovering and straightening out just before the first jump in the line. Alyssa was distracted. Her dad was MIA and it was affecting her riding.

Brynlei knew it was horrible, but she wished Alyssa would make just one small mistake. If Bentley chipped in or Alyssa jumped ahead, Brynlei would win the blue ribbon in the 3' Hunters. Alyssa would most likely still win Top Rider, but at least Brynlei would have a small taste of success.

After the line, Alyssa sat up and slowed Bentley to a steady pace in the corner. They began their approach to large yellow-and-green oxer. Three strides to go. Anyone could see the distance, but Alyssa wasn't focusing on her strides or the jump; she was looking up at the bleachers, at the empty space where her dad was supposed to be sitting.

Then, they were two strides out. One stride. Alyssa wasn't concentrating on the jump ahead of her. By the time she asked Bentley to jump, it was too late. Out of confusion, Bentley attempted to clear the oxer at the last second, but they were too close to the enormous obstacle by then. Bentley twisted in the air, crashing through the poles, his front legs snapping one of the poles in half like a twig. The crash jarred Alyssa from the saddle and sent her flying into the air before she hit the ground, face first.

It all happened in a split-second, yet it seemed to play in slow motion before Brynlei's eyes. The twisting horse, the snapping PVC pole, the broken pole's razor edge slicing across Bentley's leg, Alyssa hitting the ground like a sack of flour. Then the gasps of horror from the bleachers pierced by screams from Alyssa's mom. Alyssa's dad emerged from the office and looked around as if he was lost. Slowly, his face registered what had just happened, what he'd missed while on his business call. He let the office door slam behind him and sprinted toward the ring, a few seconds behind his wife.

Bruce was already there, holding Bentley by the reins, a pool of blood forming in the sand. Miss Jill helped Alyssa sit up, brushing the sandy dirt from her breeches and hunt coat. Alyssa looked even more stunned than the onlookers, as she spit a mouthful of sand from her mouth. Her parents ran to her, but she pushed past them and limped over to Bentley. Tears streamed down Alyssa's face as soon as she saw the injury to Bentley's front leg. Debbie ran over to witness the severity of the injury for herself, the huge gash, the white tendon visible behind the layers of severed flesh.

"Oh dear. It might be a tendon." She ran to the office to call Foxwoode's vet. After a couple minutes she returned to the group, her lips pursed together. "Our usual vet was called to the trailer accident outside the show in Traverse City. Two of his customer's horses were in the trailer that flipped over. It's going to be at least four hours until they can get here. They said our alternate vet is over there, too."

"We can't wait that long." Alyssa's face was smeared with dirt and tears. Bentley hung his head low, and Alyssa buried her face in his neck.

"She's right," Bruce said. "This looks bad."

"I have another number," Debbie said. She raced back to the office to call a different vet. After a minute, she jogged back to the tense cluster of people surrounding the injured horse. "They're not answering. It keeps ringing and ringing."

Alyssa's dad stepped in front of Debbie. "Call someone else. Do you have any idea how much money I've spent on this horse? Get a vet here!" He spoke like someone who was used to getting his way.

"I'm trying, sir," Debbie said, not backing down. "These horses mean everything to us."

"What about McMahon?" Tom asked. "He's been out here before." For a moment, Tom succeeded in diverting Alyssa's dad's wrath from Debbie to himself.

"Their office is an hour away, but that's better than four hours," Debbie said.

"I'll call him," Tom said.

The anxious onlookers watched as Tom lumbered toward the office, as fast as his tree trunk legs would carry him. Minutes later, he returned with the same awkward stride.

"There was no answer. I left a message to call back immediately. I'm heading back so I'll be there when they call. I'll come when I hear anything."

No one spoke, but Debbie locked eyes with him and nodded. With that, Tom turned and lumbered back to the office, sweat soaking through the back of his shirt in uneven patches.

Time ticked by, the bloody puddle in the sand spreading beneath Bentley. Tom did not return. Miss Jill retrieved the first aid kit from the barn and wrapped some gauze around Bentley's leg to slow the blood loss, but the blood quickly consumed the clean white gauze, turning it red. A crowd gathered around the perimeter of the ring. McKenzie stood nearby with her parents, crying.

"He's losin' a heck of a lot of blood," Bruce said. "He needs sutures."

Brynlei felt her heart being ripped from her chest as Bentley suffered in front of her. She had never wanted this to happen. Was it her fault? She'd wished for Alyssa to mess up, but she didn't mean like this. The secret in the woods weighed heavily on Brynlei.

Surely, Caroline, with all of her training, would know what to do. Caroline could save Bentley. No. It wasn't an option. Caroline would be starting her new life in a matter of days. Brynlei had made a promise not to tell, had given her word. Would Caroline want a horse to die because of her secret? Brynlei didn't think so. Still, it would be too big of a sacrifice to ask of Caroline. She'd managed to stay hidden for this long and was about to be free, a world of possibilities before her. Plus, Caroline and Bruce could go to jail. Brynlei didn't want it to be her decision.

Bentley began swaying back and forth, legs stumbling, trying to lie down.

"Where's the vet?" Alyssa's dad yelled.

Alyssa sobbed loudly. For once, it wasn't an act.

"I'll go check with Tom and report back," Miss Jill said.

Debbie didn't respond to Miss Jill, her watery eyes taking in the sight of the impaired horse. Debbie was not in a state of mind to disagree with anyone. Beads of sweat hung on her upper lip and forehead. Miss Jill sprinted toward the office while the rest of the group waited for someone to rescue Bentley, a rescue that seemed to be further and further out of reach.

Brynlei looked at Bruce, her eyes pleading with his. He knew what she was asking of him. Is Caroline's secret worth the life of this horse? Would she want it to be? Bruce's eyes held onto Brynlei, tighter than the rope that had bound her wrists. Brynlei waited for a signal—a nod of the head, a wave of the hand.

Bruce gave nothing away. He remained expressionless, stone-faced.

His loyalty was to Caroline above all else.

Bentley's front legs buckled just before his massive body sunk into the sand. An agonizing scream escaped from Alyssa, as she desperately tried to pull him back up. Others joined to help.

Brynlei's stomach flipped upside down, and the dark energy pressed in on her. She heard people talking around her, but could not make out the words. A cold sweat covered her body as she fought to breathe. She couldn't take it. The night she watched the deer die, she'd promised herself she'd never be responsible for the suffering of another animal. Caroline could save Bentley.

Outside of Bruce, Brynlei was the only one who knew. She had no choice. She led Jett to the mounting block, tightened his girth, and climbed on. Amid the chaos, she blended into the background. Bruce's face hardened as a flame of realization flickered in his eyes. He shook his head.

"No, Brynlei," he yelled.

His sudden outburst drew the attention of the others. Everyone turned to look at Brynlei who now sat aboard Jett.

"I'm going to get help," Brynlei called out. Bruce's eyes narrowed. Debbie and the others stared in confusion. Brynlei dug her heels into Jett's sides. As she and Jett raced away, she glanced back at the crowd of people with their mouths agape. A moment later, she and Jett were swallowed by the woods.

Chapter Sixteen

They galloped through the forest, weaving in and out of trees, as if threading a thousand needles. Brynlei perched in the saddle with Caroline positioned just behind, holding onto Brynlei's waist with one arm and her veterinary kit with the other.

It hadn't taken her long to find Caroline in her hidden cabin, now that she knew where to go. A few knocks on the wooden hatch had brought Caroline out of her hiding place, a confused look on her face when she saw Brynlei standing before her. She had imagined Caroline would need time to decide what to do, to weigh the cost of helping the horse against the chance for a fresh start at her life as Jane Carlisle. To Brynlei's surprise, Caroline did not hesitate, except to ask about the severity of Bentley's injury. As Brynlei described the injury to the horse's leg, Caroline had immediately recognized the urgency of the situation and gathered the necessary supplies. Brynlei had stared at her, silent with awe, as Caroline buckled her veterinary kit closed and pulled her hair back in a ponytail.

"Are you sure you want to do this?"

Brynlei was the one who had had second thoughts. Caroline had so much to lose. Bruce could go to jail. It suddenly hadn't seemed fair to ask this of her.

"I don't want to. I have to. Let's go. We don't have time to waste."

Caroline's words had jolted Brynlei back to the task at hand. The decision had been made. Just like that.

They emerged from the safety of the woods to the competing sounds of Alyssa sobbing and her dad screaming at Debbie, threatening a lawsuit that would ruin Foxwoode for eternity. The sunlight shocked

Brynlei's eyes and she squinted to adjust. Caroline's nervous energy enveloped Brynlei, so that she, herself, could barely breathe. What must Caroline be feeling at this moment? How frightened must she be? Brynlei wished that in her next life she could be half as brave as Caroline.

She pulled Jett to a halt at the entrance of the ring and Caroline swung herself to the ground. Brynlei couldn't look at Bruce, who remained standing next to Bentley. She'd gone back on her word. They'd managed to get Bentley back on his wavering feet while she'd been gone. Caroline rushed to his side.

How long would it take for someone to realize the identity of the mysterious vet from the woods? Surely, the stunning green eyes and long black hair would give her away. Caroline did not waste any time. She removed the syringe from her kit and began flushing out Bentley's wound with saline. Bentley leaned all his weight to the right, favoring his good leg. Alyssa held Bentley's head in her arms and watched Caroline work. Even Alyssa's dad stopped yelling long enough to observe Caroline's purposeful treatment of the wound.

"Why didn't you get her out here before?" Alyssa's dad shouted.

Debbie studied the woman whisked from the woods to treat Bentley, as if she knew her from somewhere. Debbie's face bubbled with confusion as she looked back and forth from Brynlei to Caroline to the woods. Then Debbie made the impossible realization, her eyes stretching wide and her mouth hanging open.

"For the love of God." Debbie spoke the words under her breath, but Brynlei heard.

Debbie grabbed Tom's arm and whispered something in his ear. Then it was Tom's turn to look like he'd just seen a ghost. He stood completely still, staring at Caroline, the color drained from his face.

"Caroline? Is that you?" Debbie spoke softly, as if she was afraid of scaring Caroline back into the woods, of losing her again.

Caroline flashed her brilliant green eyes directly at Debbie, but didn't say a word. She began the process of suturing the wound closed with a giant needle and thread that looked like dental floss.

Everyone had heard Debbie's question. A wave of whispers swept through the crowd, tomorrow's headlines ebbing and flowing from one person to the next. Bruce stood in the middle of the swirling tides, like a lighthouse refusing to budge. His eyes looked sad, resigned. Caroline would not make it to her new life as Jane Carlisle after all, but Bruce was still there for her. He had her back. Brynlei knew that if he had to go to jail for her, he would.

Caroline ignored the buzzing crowd around her and continued sewing the horse's torn flesh back together. Her work wasn't crude, as Brynlei imagined it would be. The stitches were uniform and perfectly spaced. Bentley lifted his leg every few seconds, and Caroline waited patiently for him to lower it before continuing. Caroline pulled sheets of non-stick gauze from her kit and wrapped it gently around Bentley's leg, followed by thick cotton sheeting. The blood no longer soaked through. Caroline gently secured it all with a wrap-around bandage.

"You'll need to keep this soft cast on him until he can be seen by a real vet," Caroline told Alyssa. "He'll need some anti-inflammatory medication too, like Phenylbutazone. I don't have any or I'd give it to him now."

Alyssa nodded. "Thank you. Is he going to be okay?"

"He should be," Caroline said. "He lost a lot of blood and he has a tendon injury, so he'll need several weeks of rest."

While Caroline was absorbed in her task of treating Bentley's leg, Debbie edged closer to the office, fading to the background. Brynlei followed a few steps behind and peered through the window as Debbie quietly lifted the phone to her ear and dialed a number.

* * * *

The crowd inched closer to Caroline, each person wanting to see for themselves the girl who had been missing for the last four years. Most of them had never met Caroline, but were familiar with her tragic story. After all, it had been all over the news for months after she disappeared. Every girl who attended Foxwoode learned of Caroline's story at some point during her stay, whether from a bonfire ghost story, as Brynlei had, or as an explanation for the myriad of safety precautions that Foxwoode required.

"Caroline? Is that really you?" a man yelled from the crowd.

"Are you okay? Did someone kidnap you?" McKenzie's mother

asked.

Caroline stood motionless next to Bruce, surveying the crowd. Her glance sliced into each of them, challenging them even to try to attempt to understand what she'd been through.

Brynlei's parents begged her for an explanation. How did she know where Caroline Watson was? Where had she gone to find her?

"It's not my story to tell." She repeated the line again and again, until her parents finally stopped asking questions.

"Well, you're going to have to talk to the police." Brynlei's mom sighed in exasperation as she looked in the direction of three police cruisers zooming toward them. They appeared like a stampede in a cloud of dust and flashing lights.

The chief of police ushered Caroline into the back of his car. "No handcuffs are necessary," he told Caroline. "We just want to know where you've been the last four years."

Another officer led Bruce into the back seat of the second cruiser. Apparently, they suspected him of something after seeing how Caroline refused to leave his side.

Brynlei was next. "I'm Officer Crowley," said a third policeman, whose extra weight and drooping mustache gave him the appearance of a walrus. He told her parents that one of them could ride in the patrol car with her and the other could follow them to the station.

"We need to ask some questions of your daughter regarding how she found Caroline Watson."

He didn't need to explain. Everyone wanted to know how she rode off into the woods and came back with a girl who'd been missing for four years on the back of her horse.

The police station was cold and stark. Flickering florescent lights hung at intervals from a drop tile ceiling. Voices echoed like bouncing balls off the gray cement walls and floors. There seemed to have been no room in the police budget in the last twenty years for any cosmetic improvements.

Brynlei's parents and Derek were allowed in the room with her during questioning. Officer Crowley asked her to start from the beginning. Brynlei didn't know what to do other than tell the truth. She didn't know what Caroline and Bruce were going to say, but she figured there wasn't much more she could do to protect Caroline. Caroline's secret was out and Brynlei was in enough trouble already.

She told the walrus-like police officer everything she could remember, starting from the wrong turn down the service drive. She left out the part about Bruce swinging a knife at her. There was no need to cause him any more problems.

Everyone listened intently to Brynlei's story. Even Derek barely dared to blink as the words spewed from her mouth. With each secret she revealed, a weight lifted off her back. The heavy burden of the secret she'd been carrying was removed, brick by brick. She almost felt as if she could float away. For a second, she thought it might be possible to drift back to her ordinary life in Franklin Corners as if nothing had ever happened. When there was nothing left to tell, Officer Crowley thanked her for her cooperation.

"You've been very helpful, Brynlei. Before you go, I have to ask." Officer Crowley turned his sagging body to her parents. "Would you like to press charges against Bruce Haslow for kidnapping your daughter?"

Brynlei's eyes almost popped out of her head. "No. He didn't hurt me. He just tied my hands together for a few minutes so I'd listen to Caroline's story." Brynlei stared at her parents, silently pleading.

"I don't think charges are necessary," her dad said. "At least, not as far as Brynlei is concerned."

"Very well. We'll call you if we need to talk to Brynlei again." As Officer Crowley led them out of the room, a woman barged through the door at the end of the hallway.

"Is my daughter really here? Caroline?" Brynlei recognized Janet McDaniel from the pictures she'd seen online. Only in person, Janet's face looked more faded, her eyes even more defeated.

Officer Crowley knocked on the door of an adjoining interrogation room.

"Caroline, your mother is here."

Caroline appeared in the doorway, no emotion visible on her face. Janet rushed to her and flung herself around the daughter she'd thought she'd never see again.

"It's really you! I thought you were dead. Oh, thank God! Thank God." Tears of joy streaked Janet's face.

Overcome with emotion, she clung to her daughter as if Caroline were a lone raft floating in a tumultuous ocean of joy and grief. Caroline hugged her back, seemingly relieved that her mother greeted her with love instead of anger. Every few seconds, Janet pulled away and studied her daughter's face before smothering her in another tight hug.

"I'm sorry. I'm sorry." Janet continued to repeat the words. Was she truly aware of the damage she had done to Caroline? Did she finally realize her betrayal was the cause of her daughter's disappearance?

"Where is the man that did this to you?" Janet stared at the closed door to the third interrogation room, her tearful eyes turning wild. "He's going to pay!"

"No one did this to me, mother." Caroline pulled away from her. "I disappeared to get away from Steve." She paused. "And you. Bruce saved my life. I would have died in the woods without him."

"You would have returned to us without him." Janet's voice was laced with anger. "The police told me everything. He knew exactly where you were and he didn't report it to anyone. He kept you hidden for four years while your family agonized every second over what happened to you. I thought you were dead!"

"That was the point." Caroline's words slapped her mother in the face.

Janet bit her bottom lip and shook her head. "How could you have done that to me? To us? Steve was devastated. He led two searches for you."

"Because he was worried I'd tell someone what he did to me!" Caroline shouted the words into her mother's face. She wasn't backing down.

Janet stood up taller. "I'm not going to let you drag a good man's name through the mud just because he's dead."

Caroline's eyes searched her mother, but came up empty.

"You got what you wanted—plenty of money from Foxwoode. I hope they make you return every cent. Leave me alone and let me live my life." Caroline spun away from her mother, her face splotchy with redness.

Officer Crowley and the police chief stepped forward, trying to diffuse the situation.

"Officer," Janet said, assuming a tone of authority. "I presume you plan on pressing charges against Bruce Haslow?"

"We're looking into it ma'am. At a minimum, he obstructed a police investigation."

"Well, I hope you'll pursue kidnapping charges against him." Janet stared at Caroline. "And look into statutory rape."

"Mom, no!" Caroline squealed like an injured animal. "It wasn't like that. He's the only person who's ever helped me."

Janet raised her hand to Caroline's face, signaling her to stop. "Someday you'll understand."

Officer Crowley interjected. "Unfortunately, Caroline may face charges, too. Although they'll likely treat her as a minor."

Janet's face froze. Then she shook her head. "I guess it serves her right."

Caroline buried her head in her hands. Brynlei reached over and placed a hand on Caroline's shoulder, squeezing gently. Brynlei wanted her to know that she wasn't alone.

The police chief led a stoic Bruce from the interrogation room. Bruce walked like a robot, eyes fixed straight ahead, hands cuffed behind his back. Brynlei forced herself to look at him, but her face grew hotter with each step he took toward her. She had betrayed him. Next to her, Caroline collapsed, sobbing on the cold tile floor.

"I'm sorry," Brynlei said, her voice squeaking like a mouse.

"I'm sorry," Caroline wailed. "I couldn't let the horse die."

"You did what you thought was right. I can't blame you." There was no anger in Bruce's voice. "I'm gonna be fine." He stopped walking. "Just one thing."

"What? Anything!" Caroline pleaded.

"Keep an eye on Ranger for me." Bruce's eyes welled with tears at the mention of his loyal dog.

"Of course. When you get out I'll return him to you, happy and healthy."

Bruce nodded, as he was led outside into a throng of reporters and flashing cameras.

* * * *

Brynlei's parents drove from the police station back to Foxwoode. A heavy silence filled the car.

"Did that really just happen?" Derek asked.

"Yeah, it did." She couldn't tell if her parents were mad at her for breaking so many of Foxwoode's rules or proud of her for doing the right thing. It seemed like they hadn't decided yet.

"Let's get your bags and go home. It's been a long day." Her mom smoothed back a strand of flyaway hair.

They pulled up next to Cabin 5. Almost everyone had left Foxwoode and Brynlei's belongings were the only ones left in the cabin. She'd missed the goodbyes and the hugs and fake tears, which was fine with her. The only person she really wanted to say goodbye to, besides Miss Jill, was Anna. Brynlei had already missed that boat. A blue ribbon, two red ribbons, and a yellow ribbon, lay on top of her suitcase with a note.

You won the 3' Hunters. Congrats. Hope to see you next summer.
Miss Jill

Under normal circumstances, she would have been thrilled to beat Alyssa and win the blue ribbon in the 3' Hunters, but nothing about this day had been normal. Now the blue ribbon seemed like a silly afterthought.

As her parents and brother began loading her things into the trunk, she told them she needed to say goodbye to Jett. Brynlei walked across Foxwoode's grounds, memorizing the vision of the barn surrounded by grazing horses in the lush green pastures. She burned the scenery into her mind so she could return to it whenever she needed it. This was her happy place.

She found Jett munching on some hay in his paddock. As she approached, he looked up at her and perked his ears. He lowered his head, allowing her to hug his neck and rest her face against his. She would remember this too, his warm breath on her skin and the musty, earthy smell of his coat. Tears formed in the corners of her eyes. How could she say goodbye to this horse who was clearly perfect for her?

He was for sale, as were all the horses at Foxwoode, but there was no point asking her parents about that. She already knew the answer.

Brynlei peered through her tears into Jett's impossibly large brown eyes. She wished she could see down into the depths of those eyes, to comprehend everything this horse already understood. Jett held her gaze and looked at her as if to say, "It's okay. Everything is exactly as it should be." Brynlei had never witnessed a more breathtaking sight.

Chapter Seventeen

Brynlei called Anna the morning after she arrived home from Foxwoode. Now that Caroline's secret was out, she didn't have to hide anything from Anna. She was thankful for that. She recounted every detail from the time Anna was sent home.

"Holy crap," Anna repeated, over and over again. "You were right."

She was pleasantly surprised when Anna called her again the next day.

"Guess who I just got off the phone with?" Anna's voice teemed with excitement.

"Who?"

"Debbie Olson. She called to apologize for the misunderstanding with the vodka. She said that they'd love to have me come back next summer, free of charge and..." Anna paused for dramatic effect.

"What?"

"She said I won Top Rider. Can you believe it?"

"What? That's awesome! Congratulations. You totally deserve it." Brynlei meant it. The Olsons had never announced the winner of the Top Rider award at the show because of all of the drama that ensued after Bentley's injury. They would have given it to Alyssa by default if Anna hadn't been back in the running.

"So I'll see you at Foxwoode next summer, right?" Anna said.

"Yes. I mean, assuming my parents let me."

"I guess I'll just write to you then." They both exploded with laughter.

* * * *

Shortly after her second phone call with Anna, Brynlei's phone buzzed again.

"I hope you don't mind that I'm calling." Caroline sounded nervous on the other end of the line. "I thought you might want an update."

"Yes. I mean, no. I don't mind. Yes, I do want an update." The words fell out of Brynlei's mouth in a tangled mess. She was touched that Caroline had saved her cell phone number and that she actually bothered to call. Then again, it wasn't like Caroline had many people she could trust.

"The Olsons are letting me stay at Foxwoode until I get back on my feet. They've been great. Debbie is even helping me get together some college applications."

"That's really good news, Caroline." She couldn't help but notice that Caroline did not mention her mother.

"I had my court hearing yesterday."

Brynlei stopped breathing. "What happened?"

"They charged me as a minor because I was only fifteen when I planted the evidence and faked my death. I'm on probation for six months. That's it." Brynlei could almost hear Caroline smiling through the phone. "I'm going to take Bruce's place as the barn hand. Just until he comes back. The Olsons hired an attorney for Bruce and the police dropped most of the charges against him, except for the obstruction of justice one. The attorney says Bruce should be able to reach an agreement. He'll probably be out in six months or less."

"Oh, that's great." A wave of relief washed over Brynlei.

Six months in prison was a whole lot better than life behind bars or the death penalty. Her imagination had been running wild since she saw Bruce being led away in handcuffs. She still felt that she had somehow caused all this.

"I'm sure Ranger misses him."

Caroline laughed. "Yeah, he sure does. You probably heard that Bentley is recovering well. The Olsons heard from Alyssa's parents yesterday."

"Oh, thank God." Brynlei breathed another sigh of relief. It wasn't all for nothing. "Have you started riding again?"

"Every day. I didn't realize how much I missed it." Caroline paused again. "Brynlei, thank you for helping me."

"I'm not sure I really helped you, but you're welcome."

"Because of you I don't have to live the rest of my life as Jane Carlisle. And I'm not scared anymore. I can be myself."

"I'm happy for you, Caroline." A smile spread across Brynlei's face. "Maybe in your next life your name will be Jane Carlisle."

An awkward silence hung on the line.

"That was a joke," Brynlei explained. "I believe in past lives … and future lives, I guess."

"Oh. I get it. That's funny."

"Anyway, will you call me if anything happens with Bruce? Or if you just want to talk?"

"Yeah. We'll keep in touch. Hopefully I'll see you at Foxwoode next summer."

"Yes. I think you will." Brynlei knew she'd find a way to go back.

* * * *

Brynlei sat on her bed at home and traced her finger around one of the squares on the patchwork quilt. Rebecca lounged on the matching twin bed opposite her. She'd returned from Interlochen the day before. Brynlei told her to get comfortable. The story was going to take a while.

"Well, now my violin camp seems really lame." Rebecca sighed. "I didn't see any ghosts or find any missing girls. I just practiced violin with a bunch of other nerdy teenagers."

Brynlei smiled. "I'm sure you had fun though, right? I mean, you probably made some new friends."

"Yeah, but no one with blue hair."

"You'll like Anna. She kind of reminds me of you."

"Me with blue hair?"

Brynlei laughed at the thought. Even Rebecca couldn't pull that off. She continued answering all of Rebecca's questions about the mysterious tale of Caroline Watson, but the buzz of Brynlei's cell phone interrupted them. The screen lit up with the words, "Can I take u to dinner on Friday?"

"It's Luke!" Brynlei squealed, relieved that he hadn't suggested the zoo.

173

"What does it say? What does it say?" Rebecca grabbed the phone out of her hand and started hooting like a maniac.

"Lover boy wants to take you to dinner. You must have really wowed him with your bowling skills." Rebecca started typing a message into the phone.

"What are you doing?" Brynlei's mouth gaped open. She could only imagine what inappropriate message Rebecca had just sent to Luke.

"Relax, Sherlock."

Brynlei grabbed the phone back and saw the word *Yes* below Luke's message.

"I feel like I'm going to throw up." She flopped back on her bed.

This was it. She was going on a real first date with a boy she actually liked. There was no turning back, thanks to Rebecca. It was time to stop hiding beneath the surface. Time to step out of her comfort zone and take a risk, put herself out there. That was the only way to move forward in life. She'd learned that much from Caroline.

"What if I don't have anything to talk about?"

"Um, given the story you've just been telling me for the last hour, I don't think that's going to be a problem."

Brynlei smiled. Rebecca was right. It was a good story.

About the Author

Laura Wolfe lives in her home state of Michigan with her husband, son, and daughter. She holds a BA in English from the University of Michigan and a JD from DePaul University. Her writing has been published in multiple magazines, including Practical Horseman.

Laura is an accomplished English rider and a lover of animals and nature. When she is not writing, she can be found playing games with her highly-energetic kids, growing vegetables in her garden, or spoiling her rescue dog. She dreams of living in a log cabin on a minimum of one hundred acres, ideally, in a slightly warmer climate.

Contact Information:

www.AuthorLauraWolfe.com
www.Facebook.com/AuthorLauraWolfe

Acknowledgments

So many people supported and encouraged me during the very long process of writing this book. I'd like to extend a special thanks to my husband, JP, and my children, Brian and Kate, who never once doubted me; to Ana Wolfe, Karina Board, Torrey Lewis, Megan Cleere, and Kelly Hashway, for reading the early drafts and providing valuable feedback; to my brother, Dave Peterson, for lending his awesome editing skills on very short notice; to my parents, for instilling a love of books in me from a very young age; and to the editors at Fire and Ice, for taking a chance on my first novel. I am forever grateful!